DOWN INTO THE SEA

DOWN INTO THE SEA

DAN FRANKLIN

CEMETERY DANCE PUBLICATIONS

Baltimore

2024

Cemetery Dance Publications
132B Industry Lane, Unit #7
Forest Hill, MD 21050
www.cemeterydance.com

Trade Paperback Edition

ISBN:
978-1-58767-985-8

Dedicated to my wife Kelsey
and my children, Layla and Marshall
To those who will never be satisfied
And to all those who transform.

"There are three sorts of people:
those who are alive,
those who are dead,
and those who are at sea."

—— Anacharsis

CHAPTER ONE:

The Tilt-a-Whirl spun him around in a dizzying blur and Eric Ross clenched his jaw, forced his eyes to stay open against the bitter September wind.

Each sight gave reluctant submission to the next, snapshot images locking into place before they were torn away and he scrambled for a new mental foothold. The polished brass of the carousel, peaked in medieval pennants of yellows, greens, purples. The cloud-cut twilight sky above a dull ocean horizon with water the color of slate. Faces, too. Other teenagers, their eyes wide and mouths gaping in laughter, in speaking, in screams that never quite reached him.

The ride gave a labored creak as it slowed and the pitted foam on the safety bar pressed against his hips. His stomach churned. When he could at last pull himself free, he fumbled toward the weather-beaten wooden railing even before his feet had fully found their strength. Sensations spilled back to him, one by one.

First, the smells. The salt of the ocean, the heavy yellow weight of stale popcorn and spilled beer, of greased metal and the cloying, rotten sweetness of cotton candy.

Sounds came next—a carnival reel, tinny and high and mechanical, the squeaks of half-rusted gears, the weary grind and clack of the Tilt-a-Whirl powering back up, the shrieks from the swinging pirate ship ride. A radio cranked up to its highest, blasting out pop music down at the end of the pier beside the light-bulb-studded Ferris wheel. The hurried, conspiratorial giggling of older teens pawing at each other on the Lover's Bench as the carousel churned by in front of them.

His fingers dug into the railing, nails pressing furrows into the soft, wind-smoothed pine as he coached himself through deep, slow breaths, catching and releasing the subtle promise of ice that never quite left the New England air. Little by little, the world ceased its dervish tilting and he could stand without helplessly tumbling to the side. His hair hung down in front his face, long and greasy and damp. He pushed it back.

In through your nose, out through your mouth.

His father's voice, almost as if the man was there with him instead of locked away in some cell up in Cedar Junction. He swallowed down the urge to vomit. His dad wouldn't have thrown up.

A few dozen feet below, the gray ocean sloshed against the rocky Massachusetts beach, swirled around the stork-like wooden legs of the entertainment pier.

And there she was.

It took him a moment to realize she was real, and there, and not some trick of his mind.

A body, his imagination whispered. *A corpse.*

Not that bodies ever washed up. There were occasional drownings, of course, but the sea always dragged them out. It was something of a local point of pride, in Coleridge.

She drifted through the water on her back, naked chested and ghostly pale, colorless hair pooled around her in a waterlogged halo. Any hint of her legs was lost beneath the water and the shadow cast by the pier. The distance made it hard to tell, but Eric thought she might be smiling.

He stared at her in absolute awe.

In his fourteen years he'd never seen anything like it, could barely process what he was looking at until her eyes flickered open and focused on him. The maybe-smile vanished and the look on her face stirred something primal in him, an instinctive, atavistic dread. She was *wrong*. Wrong in how she moved, wrong in how she looked.

He raised his hand in timid greeting.

A flicker of green rolled through her hair, a subtle glowstick shimmer that vanished as quickly as it came, and then she slipped under into the shroud of waves.

He waited for her to surface. She did not.

He stayed waiting until Mr. Yarrow left the carousel's control podium and came to stand next to him.

"Eric," he said. A dark-skinned mountain of a man in flannel and suspenders, Mr. Yarrow ran the Bay Point Pier, every bit as inseparable a part of it as the rides themselves. He chewed, leaned carefully over the side and spat a brown splatter of tobacco juice into the water below.

Eric wanted to tell him not to, but the woman was already gone. If she had ever been there at all. The more he thought about it, the less likely it seemed.

"Hey, Mr. Yarrow."

"Son. Might want to get scarce." He nodded his head back down the pier, not to the motley collection of rides, but to the boy in the brown leather jacket who rose head and shoulders above the others.

Eric followed his gesture and flinched.

There were three of them strolling side by side with a proprietorial confidence, as if they owned both the pier and the September night itself.

The tall one was Brandon Anders. The other two were Mr. Yarrow's son Christian and a perpetually sunburned blonde kid named Handsy—although his real name was some Norwegian mess that no one could pronounce. Christian and Handsy were Eric's age and neither were trouble on their own, but Brandon… The three picked their way down the pier, laughing into the night, lost in the lights and sounds and life for a moment. They had become more or less inseparable ever since Eric's dad had shot Brandon's brother in the head.

A corpse.

Eric wasn't surprised to see them, but it gave him a nasty jolt just the same. He rubbed at the back of one arm, felt the scabs of half healed cigarette burns from the last time Brandon had caught up with him.

Coleridge didn't afford much for fun beside the Bay Point Pier. A fishing town that had lingered long after the local industry had died and a tourist trap for those who wanted to avoid the bustle and pricetags of Gloucester, Coleridge had become steadily less of either and more of a stopping point for truckers who got diverted off onto Route 6. Eric's dad used to complain about the eighteen wheelers, spent most of his week in his police cruiser either pulling them over or chasing off the drunken college students who spilled over from Rhode Island.

"Thanks, Mr. Yarrow," he said.

The big man grunted, wiped tobacco juice from his beard, and headed back toward the carousel to start it up again for its next circuit.

Eric leaned against the railing, skirting the shadows as he waited. When the three boys stopped at one of the booths to heft weighted baseballs toward stacked vintage milk bottles, he slipped by.

It was easy enough to blend in with the scattered crowds. On the pier, he was just another teenager, underfed and freckled and dirty, his dark hair too long and constantly crowding across his face, dressed in a t-shirt when the tourists were already wearing snow coats. No one noticed him. No one pulled away. Out on the pier he was like all those other kids who didn't have a dad who shot a boy to death. For a moment, he felt free.

He made his way past the game shacks and bustling food stands and out into the parking lot, to the metal waves of the bike rack beside it.

Out from beneath the canopy of Christmas lights, Eric could see the sky was a mottle of bruised purples, the sun having long since abandoned its heights. The entrance to the pier was designed to look something vaguely like a castle gate, and he kept an eye on the gateway as he crouched down beside his Schwinn.

The bike had seen better days. He'd won it three years ago at bingo, back when he did things like bingo, but living near the ocean took a toll. He unhooked the lock and rethreaded the bicycle chain through the teeth of the weary gears until the wheel spun in time with the pedals. Then he paused.

He should go home.

There was no sense in lingering around to see if Brandon and the others had noticed him. Out on the pier, they might have roughed him up a bit, but with the privacy of the parking lot and the sun set, it would be that much worse.

There was nothing new to see, anyway. The light was fading. All that was left was for Mr. Yarrow to start kicking the last wave of visitors out. Then he would walk the Bay Point, whistling in time with whatever song the radio spat out as he inspected each ride for any damages and dragged any remaining stragglers to the front. The lights stayed on, even when autumn gathered enough momentum and the rides closed until spring. When he killed the music, the night was finished.

Closing time was as reliable as clockwork. Eric had watched it probably a hundred times in the past half a year. The rides were already small, shrunken down to keep from collapsing the pier, and the bearded man towered among them like some sort of flannel-wearing Godzilla patrolling his turf of garish flags and old wood and tented strands of Christmas lights.

Eric had tried drawing the sunset over the pier, but there was an otherworldly quality to it all that defied capture.

Instead, tonight, he found himself looking over toward the staircase.

He wondered if she was still out there.

The stairs—called the Suicide Steps by most kids—led down the rocky cliff face as they dipped toward the surf. Damp wooden planks had been bolted among chipped rock chunks the size of heads of lettuce, gravel crowding into any gaps in the salt-frosted stone.

He *should* go home, and yet...

The steps had no gate and no safety rail, relying instead on the dubious prospect of a dented warning sign and common sense to keep most people away, so Eric had no trouble slipping out onto them. Each step down toward the beach grew noticeably colder, each plank progressively slicker and more saturated with the sea water below. The smell of popcorn and corndogs and sweat gave way to a rotten, fishy smell of aquatic decay and the hint of garbage fallen from the pier above.

Darkness reigned in the shadows below the pier, a pocket of winter and night below all that festive life. The murmur of voices, the radio and the circus music reached out from above but seemed to only highlight the divide.

He shuffled his feet, kicked against the pebbles, scattered water-smoothed stones among the flecks of dirty sand. In the twilit shadows, they all amounted to the same frigid beige blur. The consensus that blue was the color for cold was a sham, and anyone who'd grown up near a beach in Massachusetts knew it. The choppy gray of the Atlantic was cold. The cracked quartz and limestone, dolomite and basalt striated with otherworldly white streaks all spelled out an icy bitterness that would infiltrate your blood. Browns, blacks, whites—all those flesh hues laid out, bare and worn by the salt and sea—those were the real colors of cold.

Eric wrapped his arms around himself and felt like an idiot as he watched the slow surge and pull of the water among the wooden posts that supported the pier like a forest of leafless bark-less trees, each thicker around than he was. They couldn't even afford proper breakers in Coleridge, his dad used to joke.

There wasn't much to see. Dirt and grit caked the rocky face of the cliff, peppered with paper bags and broken bottles. Half-columns sprouted from the water beside the shallower support pilings, capped in beaten metal as often as not, remnants from piers that had come before the Bay Point. Someone had abandoned a bright blue square of a tarp on the beach, and it now cradled greasy, bug-infested puddles left by high tide. Slippery, greening rockpools studded the shore, and the sand that pushed out from beneath the carpet of pebbles glittered with broken glass and discarded fishhooks.

Even the most ardent of lovers avoided the beach beneath the pier, keeping their trysts to their parents' cars and the patches of scraggly pines up on top of the cliff. The beach was Eric's alone.

The emptiness left him nervous. He'd always avoided the desolate stretch of shoreline and he wasn't sure what he was hoping to find now. If Brandon and the others noticed him here… Whatever he had seen earlier was gone, anyway, just an illusion or a slip of his imagination. There was no naked, legless woman floating out beneath the pier. That sort of thing wasn't just impossible. It was insanity. It was a panel of doctors and pills and just one more burden when he could carry no more.

He should climb back up the stairs, head home.

The thought made him feel vaguely sick. Going crazy—*off your rocker*, his dad would have said—was easier to handle than home, so he stood and waited just one minute longer and adjusted to the gloom.

If not, he wouldn't have seen the face hunched beside the pillar, eyes staring back at him from the darkness.

"Jeezfuck Christ," he whispered. His father's old standby obscenity, summoned without thinking.

The face smiled. A dull glow flickered through her hair, a winking firefly bioluminescence that spilled light across her features. On wide, dark eyes that were too big and set with too little whites behind them. On her rounded cheeks and wide mouth. On skin pale enough to be translucent, her body a marble roadmap of veins beneath.

The smile stretched, and Eric could see a bristle of thin, jagged teeth behind her lips.

CHAPTER TWO:

His heartbeat thundered, a stammering, nauseated drumroll. He wiped the sweat from his hands. Impossible. It had to be some mistake, some trick of the light, a carving or a statue or a gruesome sort of joke. Only it was moving.

She was moving.

Not some hallucination. She had teeth and she was watching him. Hadn't there been some story about cannibals on the Maine beachfront he'd read about online?

But it wasn't that, because there was something entirely inhuman about her.

A wave of dizziness crashed over him, the pumping of his heart dredging up the Tilt-a-Whirl's vertigo until he had to squat down to catch his balance.

In through your mouth, out through your nose.

The face remained.

He raised his hand in greeting and she slowly raised her own in imitation.

Thoughts broke through his reverie in broken fragments. Nails at the end of each finger, long and sharp and hooked like talons. Between her fingers, a thin greenish webbing. The cluster of curved teeth. The weapons of a predator.

She slithered closer to the shore, cutting through the water with an effortless wriggle of her body.

He should go. He shouldn't just walk away, either. He should run.

She couldn't climb the stairs after him.

She didn't have legs.

She slipped up above the water, the rolling surf spilling around her waist, leaving her bare from her hips up. Her pale hair clung to her, drab cords that coiled across and gripped her skin like the tentacles of some otherworldly jellyfish. Eric tried his best to not gawk at the curve of her naked breasts with their dark nipples, at the forked lightning of veins that disappeared behind the layers of brine green scales that extended below her navel.

With only a few feet of water left, she stopped.

He had a sudden image of her clamoring up onto the beach, dragging herself by her hands and snapping at him like some sort of crocodile.

"Hi," he said.

He wondered if she could speak English. If she understood any of it. If she even had the capacity to understand.

She let out a wild, tumbling laugh.

"Hi. Come on and swim…"

Her accent was difficult to parse, a lilting musical rhythm at odds with her rougher voice. It sounded like a song. The firefly

glow rolled through her again, lighting constellations in her hair and gleaming in her eyes as she lingered over the notes.

Eric took a deep breath. The sharp, vaguely rotten smell of the beach helped to steady him as much as the cold. He shook his head.

"I… uh… I can't. I have to go home." He waved toward the cliff behind him and the sunset beyond. "And it's cold."

The woman in the water drifted back to the shadows beneath the pier where she leaned up against one of the supports. Flecks of the strange, nightlight glow danced through her eyes as she studied him.

"Come swim…" she began again, and hummed the next few notes.

A song. Had he heard a song like that? The dizziness had passed, but Eric still couldn't make much sense of his thoughts.

"What are you?" he asked. He knew the answer, though. He felt himself blush. "I don't mean you're like a monster or anything, I just mean…"

"Monster?"

It took him a moment to realize she was asking a question.

"Like a weird… creature or whatever. Something scary."

She pursed her lips into a pout and Eric decided that she was beautiful.

"Take off shoes."

"What?"

The playfulness left her face.

"Shoes?" she asked the word as if uncertain.

"Yeah, okay." Eric slipped his shoes off one by one, then his socks. The ground was absurdly cold, the water-smoothed pebbles like cubes of ice beneath his soles. He flexed his toes and tried not to think about the stray fishing hooks and broken glass, about his precious blood splashing and steaming on the wet sand. "Better?"

She nodded with enough enthusiasm that her wet hair swung before slapping back against her neck and shoulders. She leaned against the piling and stared at his feet with a concentration that made him wish he'd showered earlier. He tried to keep his eyes from skipping down to her cleavage as the waves passed and pulled away from her.

"It's cold. Aren't you cold?" he asked. She stared at him, no indication of understanding in her dark eyes. "You're naked."

"Nai-ked?"

"You don't have…" He tugged at his shirt.

She let go of the piling and dipped lower into the water until only her head and shoulders remained visible, bobbing along with the waves. The moment she was under, he wished she would come back out.

"Better?" she asked.

"How do you understand me, anyway?"

"I listen. Many years. Songs are easiest. Songs make everything groooovy."

She grinned like she'd told a joke. A flicker of those hideous teeth. The distant jangle of the radio above cut off, as if on cue, and she sighed.

"What's your name?" he asked. "Do you have a name?"

"R'hial."

"Reel?"

She tossed her head from side to side.

"Are." She pointed to herself "Hee. All. R'hial."

"R'hial. I'm Eric."

Her eyebrows shot up in surprise.

"R'Ic?"

"Just Eric."

She considered it and nodded.

"Justaric. You are here again? Tomorrow?"

"Again? Yeah. I'll be here again. I go to the pier a lot."

She nodded. "The pier. Why?"

Eric shrugged. He wanted desperately to find some clever answer that would impress her, but nothing came to him. "It's fun. It makes things seem… better. Even when they're bad."

She looked up at the monolithic black expanse of the pier's underside.

"Talk the pier. Slow. Now."

"Talk about the pier?"

"Now."

"There are rides. Rides are fun things that move fast. There are happy people. There are—" he almost mentioned the girls. The Lover's Bench. The subtle whisper of something he didn't quite understand, but which drew him in with unyielding force. "There's popcorn. The best popcorn you'll ever eat. In a big glass cart. All yellow and buttery and hot. Corndogs too."

"Popcorn," she murmured, turning the word over in her mouth.

"Yeah." He rummaged in the pockets of his sweatpants, found a few spare kernels and held one white puff, like the blossom of some bizarre flower, toward her. "It's food. You eat it."

She watched him for a long moment before putting her hand out palm up, fingers spread to turn the webbing into a cup.

He hitched up his pants, waited until the water pulled back, and darted forward far enough to climb onto one of the shorter, broken pilings, his feet slapping on the icy sand as he scrambled. He stretched his hand out toward her, only then realizing his mistake. He was off balance and too close. If she grabbed him and pulled, dug those talon claws into his skin… but she didn't. She stretched her hand beneath his. He dropped the kernel into her palm.

"Eat?" she asked. She sounded doubtful.

"It's food."

"Grooovy, Eric." She pronounced his name *Ahr-ic*, and when she laughed, he couldn't help but glance down at the movement of her body just beneath the water. He looked up to find her watching him.

"Thank you," she said.

She set the piece of popcorn in her mouth, chewed and made a disgusted face. She spat it out. She frowned at him. He hopped back down onto the sand and backpedaled toward the shore. His feet were half numb before he reached the rocks.

"Come on and swim?" she asked again. No humming this time, just a question. Another flicker of radiance trekked its way through her eyes and hair.

"It's night. I need to get home."

She shrugged. He wasn't sure if she understood or not, but he didn't follow up because a distant thrum resonated through his gut, a foghorn chord from somewhere out beyond the waves. She made the same face from when she had tried the popcorn.

"What is it?" he asked.

"Again, Eric," she said. "Again."

Then she turned, shook her head and dipped down into the waves. A serpentine ripple of greenish scales followed her. She popped up again a few dozen yards farther out and then she disappeared entirely.

"Wait!" he called out, but she did not surface again.

"Please don't go," he whispered.

His words fell, unheard, on the beach and like so many waves, broke, and were swept away.

CHAPTER THREE:

Sweat spilled down his face despite the night time chill and Eric pedaled harder. The rush of air tugged at him, tangled bitter, bony fingers in hair that spilled down to his shoulders. His heart pounded as he replayed the night again and again.

Impossible.

Again, Eric, she had said. *Again.*

And she had smiled.

He felt like he was flying on his Schwinn, cutting up into the night sky, like that old movie with the creepy brown alien. He'd watched it with his dad and sister and mom, back when they'd been a family, huddled together under mismatched blankets on their too-small couch. A movie from before his time and, if he were honest, a kind of shitty one at that, but the warm press of their bodies against him gave the memory a sort of religious weight.

He wanted to scream out his exhilaration as he rocketed along the interstate's sand-swept shoulder and off onto Wopanaak, but he contained it to a manic grin.

Scraggly pines stood sentry on either side of the Coleridge's main street, punctuated every so often by storm-weathered shops and restaurants, abandoned shacks and old motels with xenon-green vacancy signs and half empty parking lots. A fire house, a police station that Eric recognized all too well, a handful of laundromats and the post office. The sidewalk was cracked and pitted and weeds jutted like green fingers from the gaps. A mile later and the stores gave way to squat houses and neighborhood signs, white-paint sidings, bright doors and well-washed, aging cars.

His smile faded as he turned onto Maple Park. With each passing house, his shoulders slumped more.

Home.

The neighborhood row of nearly identical ranchers, bright-colored doors, sidewalk paths and short, even strips of manicured lawns between. Nothing fancy, but not cheap either. Eric remembered the look of pride on his mother's face as she stooped beside the thin garden out front, comically giant gloves on her tiny wrists, dirt smudged on her cheeks and chin, her mouth curved into a smile.

Each house matched, soldiers in a uniform line… and then the one exception. Tall weeds bent and shivered with the passing breeze, crickets chirped from hidden perches underneath windows that were clouded and dark. Eric wondered what would happen if the pink eviction notices ever carried out their threat. His mom promised they wouldn't. That she would get more regular work and that he shouldn't worry.

He wondered where they'd have to move. Maybe they'd end up in the trailer park next to what was left of the Anders family. The possibility left him feeling ill.

At least they wouldn't be too far from the pier.

Flat tires grumbled as he slowed and climbed down. He pawed at the matted mess of hair that spilled in front of his face. He hadn't cut it since the verdict was delivered. No one had cut their grass either. The neighbors had complained a few times, he'd heard them talk with his mother, but she hadn't done anything to change it.

If entering the neighborhood had dampened his good mood, stepping inside the house itself brought a physical, dismal weight upon him that suffocated it entirely. He wrinkled his nose at the smell as he flipped the lights on. The few remaining bulbs didn't much help. He tossed his backpack on the ground beside the door.

"I'm home," he called out, but no one answered.

His mother was sprawled out on the couch in front of the television while some anonymous reality dating show played to an audience of none. One arm and one foot dangled down to rest against the stained shag carpet. She hadn't changed out of the green polo from her shift at the gas station.

He checked on her flopped body—*a corpse?*—but of course she was alive and breathing slow and steady, her mousy hair tangled and sneakers still on. She was skinny, heading toward scarily thin, her body a collection of sticks and bones beneath skin that looked increasingly fragile. Her high cheekbones jutted. Awake, she seemed to burn inside with some hidden reserves of energy. Asleep, they guttered out.

Her mouth hung open and the yellowed whites of her eyes peeked out from beneath her loosely closed lids, but she didn't so much as stir. An orange plastic medicine bottle stood next to her on the coffee table, the safety cap popped up on one side.

He picked up the ragged blanket from where it pooled on the floor and stretched it across her like a shroud. He clicked off the television without thinking. Far from his first rodeo. If she'd taken only one pill, she might make it to bed. If she'd doubled up, she would be there until morning.

He didn't bother being quiet. There was no chance of waking her for hours yet, either way. He grabbed a piece of Wonder Bread from the bag on the kitchen counter, squeezed it into a ball, and ate it in two bites as he leaned against the old laminate countertop. The neon numbers on the stove clock counted upwards into the night as he chewed. He checked the milk, but it was a bit yellow and the chocolate syrup was still out so he drank directly from the faucet, holding his face as far above the mess as he could.

The house was a disaster.

Dishes heaped in the sink, having dumped their old cargo of mac and cheese, bread crusts and bologna flecks into an opaque pool of greasy water that never entirely drained. Papers were strewn across the kitchen table, those awful pink slips mixed in with bills, with sympathy cards, with credit card offers and advertisements that promised so much and delivered so little. Towels with cutesy slogans sewn into them—*The most important ingredient is love* and *Eat to live, live to eat*—huddled in heaps beneath the leaking fridge.

He grabbed two more pieces of bread, then headed to his room, across the tangled mess of the dirtiest of his clothes, and collapsed on his bed beneath the shadow-muffled gaze of posters that no longer mustered much interest. A geology guide from his rock phase a few years back. A collection of diagrams showing the basics of human proportions for drawing. A college pennant for UMass Dartmouth that he'd put up to appease his dad rather than from any real allegiance. Eric had always hoped to end up somewhere like MassArt where he could draw.

Back when he could bring himself to care.

He set his phone on his nightstand and stared up into the darkness as he ate the rest of the bread, bite after tasteless bite.

A mermaid.

Had it really happened? And if so... what then?

It shouldn't be possible, but reality could break. He knew that. His sister had cracked reality when she ran off to Boston with Brandon's older brother, her arms dappled in a leopard print of bruises. Her father had shattered it with two shots from his service pistol. In the wreckage, two ruined families and a dead boy.

A corpse.

But this... this was something entirely different. Now that the exhilaration had faded, he realized R'hial scared him. Damn near terrified him. If not for her nakedness, he probably would have noticed sooner.

She wasn't some gentle strawberry-haired princess, singing about her inevitable happily-ever-after. She had claws. Her laughter was wild, her eyes strange and inhuman. She had watched him with curiosity—not with the understanding of another person and certainly not with the fear of an animal.

Gentle creatures didn't have teeth like that.

He shouldn't go back. That was obvious enough. He certainly could never even tell anyone else about her. No one would believe him, and if he told someone and they somehow did, they'd have to see her for themselves. They'd intrude on his secret, they'd steal her away and ruin everything.

If he shared her.

For now, she was special. She was his.

Of course, he would go back. How could he not? She'd asked him to.

And she'd been *topless*.

He shivered, tried to hold the image in his mind.

"R'hial," he whispered. He focused on the pronunciation, practiced it again. "R'hial."

Maybe she wasn't human, or at least not like him, but so what? She was beautiful, and it wasn't like he had any real reason to want to be near people who were like him. He was scrawny, acne-faced and the girls in his class treated him with a natural disgust that he shared. Not R'hial. She'd looked at him. Had asked him to come back. He tried to imagine her naked skin against his, holding her in his arms, her sprawled out in the bed beside him. He wondered if her body would be warm or cold. He wondered how it would taste to have her mouth pressed against his own.

But when he slipped off to sleep, it wasn't the shimmer of her scales or the strange glow of her hair and eyes that filled his dreams. It wasn't the firm curve of her naked breasts or the fullness of her lips.

It was the sharpness of her teeth.

CHAPTER FOUR:

Zeke broke in onto the Bay Point Pier, the same as he usually did, his rod and tackle and cooler in tow.

If he were a few decades younger, he would have climbed over the gate, but his years as a hellraiser had long gone by. Sixty-seven, and a hard sixty-seven at that. No one had ever warned him about how stiff his hands would feel, about how his knee would sometime twinge and then not work for a day. Fortunately, the years had also left him smarter, so instead of trying something stupid he simply gave the combination lock a tug. It snapped open and he squeezed through the front gate. He pulled the gate half-closed behind himself, reached through the gap to lock it again and then shuffled his way down the darkened pier.

A mountable spotlight the size of a car battery was strapped inside his duffle, but he didn't bother reaching for it. Between the strung-up Christmas lights and the nearly full moon, there was no need. Besides, he'd been there enough times before that he could walk it with his eyes shut and he didn't really want any extra attention.

Not that there was anyone to report him. Midnight had come and gone and except for some drunken asshole weaving his way down the rocky beach below, Zeke was alone. The only sounds besides the idiot's humming were the dull rush of the water and the salt-heavy breeze that sent the pier's pennants snapping. The sky was clear enough that he could see the lights from Falmouth sparkling on the far side of Buzzard's Bay.

A perfect night for pier fishing.

Zeke had been on the ocean most of his life—first in the Navy, then on a swordfishing boat called the *Espada Rey*—but he'd never really been good at catching much besides misdemeanor sentences and diseases that left him itching between his skinny thighs.

Until he found the Bay Point.

Buzzards Bay always had a reputation for good catches, but the Bay Point Pier was something else. The men at the tackle shop said something about Falmouth shielding away most of the rough water but with enough gaps between the Elizabeth Islands that the Atlantic came through, but Zeke didn't really know. All he knew was that the fish showed up in droves.

Weird ones too. Maybe not broadbills like you could sometimes pull on a true ocean pier, but he'd pulled up rounded yellow fish with blue stripes, fish with unnaturally large, bugged out eyes, all sorts of things. Tasty suckers.

He rolled his cooler over to the carousel and set half the twelve pack on the bench.

Yarrow didn't change the locks or check up after dark or ask for permits, and Zeke left beer. The way of the world. The way things were supposed to be. You wanted it badly enough, you paid for it, you got it. He left the other six beers in the white topped cooler with the ice. There would still be enough room for any fish he caught, he supposed, and if not, well, they could flop along on top of the cans for all he cared.

Come the end of the night he'd carve off their heads and gut them and scrape off their scales with a paint mixer studded in nailed-on bottle tops. Then they'd fit easily enough. Way of the world.

He lit one of his unfiltereds as he watched the water. Scraps of froth like white linen caught the moonlight as they trundled toward the shore. He tried his best to ignore the ache in his jaw as the smoke spilled out of his mouth. A strange swelling in his throat had been growing progressively worse the last few months along-side the ache and it was beginning to make him nervous. A doctor would probably have something to say about that, but a couple extra drags helped keep him from worrying about it too much.

Too nice of a night for worrying.

As a child he had loved the night, but for most of his life since then he'd hated it. Hated being alone. Hated the quiet. Hated fishing, if he were being honest. It was just something he did out of habit and a desire to drink.

Lately, some part of his internal landscape had shifted into reverse.

He'd been spending more and more time lost in childhood memories, too. He couldn't remember what happened last week for shit, couldn't remember most of his life—although, in his defense, he was drunk through most of his time in the Navy until they dis-charged him, and it eventually cost him the *Espada Rey* job—but growing up in Coleridge back before all the sailing and suffering, the divorces and petty jail time, that part came through sharp and clear. He could feel the cold sweat of the milk box in the morning, paper crinkled up and crammed down the necks of the bottles. He could remember the scream of summer bugs, the silence of the winters. The smell of dogshit when his cocker spaniel named Bev got on the bad side of something in the pine copse over near Gidley's Corner—the same patch of trees he'd played in since he was six—and limped home with one leg torn off and let loose all over the kitchen floor. He could remember how his parents had bellowed at the dog over the mess, and how that was the day Zeke had fallen out of love with them.

He couldn't remember if he took his medication that morning, though.

He shook his head. Way of the world, he supposed. When you got to a certain age, you stopped moving forward and started sliding back. Soon enough he'd probably be shitting himself too. Wearing diapers and a bib again, mewling like a baby. He'd already lost most of his teeth. He popped the tab on one of the beers and sat his ass down on the cooler.

The drunken idiot down on the beach momentarily paused his humming to let out a magnificent belch. He could see Zeke if he cared to look, but Zeke wasn't too concerned. He wouldn't bother Zeke and Zeke wouldn't bother him. Way of the world.

"Keep your eyes to yourself and your mouth closed," he muttered to himself. "Or Ol' Chepa…"

He gave an involuntary shiver and let the sentence die.

That was a different memory. An ugly, grade school memory, from when he'd sneak away to Foreman's shack out in the pine woods. Foreman was a moonshiner, claimed to be an adopted child of the Wampanoag tribes, but no one in Zeke's crew really believed him. He was more than happy to sell to kids, though, so Zeke would spend hour after hour among the repurposed bath tubs and eyewatering stench of paint thinner listening to the old man ramble. He sold cheap and was willing to let the boys earn their drink, as long as Zeke and the other kids listened to his stories and followed his simple rule: You kept your eyes to yourself and your mouth closed.

If not, Ol' Chepa would get you. Ol' Chepa the Hobbomock.

The Hobbomock was an evil thing, a shapeshifting embodiment of brutality that slipped up into places that seemed safe and waited in ambush. A murderous entity that grabbed victims up off the side of the road or dragged them, struggling and shrieking, off of sweaty mattresses at midnight. He'd peel your eyelids right off your face. Twist your limbs in knots. Cram branches down your throat until your lungs were loose, broken bags. And with the rest of the Wampanoag's dead and dispersed, he had no friends beside Foreman. No one else to obey, or so the man whispered to his glassy-eyed, captive audience.

If anyone asked about Foreman's business or how the kids who drank for free earned their moonshine, well, you kept your eyes to yourself and your mouth closed. Or else.

Zeke could picture the crazed old man grinning, yellow-toothed, behind his filthy beard, his breath hot and reeking as they passed around jelly jars full of clear, noxious fluid. His scabby calluses pressing against Zeke's softer skin. Suddenly, the beer didn't taste all that good.

Foreman was, of course, a crazed old bastard, but the Hobbomock... well, he hadn't just come up with that one. There were deadly things out there, things that slipped into safe harbors and waited. Anyone with a lick of sense knew it to be true.

Kids really did disappear off the side of roads. Out of beds. Whether it was Ol' Chepa, or Foreman, or some bear shambling along through the pines with his dog's leg in its mouth, or even just a lump in his throat where there hadn't been six months ago, the name didn't matter.

The Hobbomock was real.

Too nice of a night for that sort of thinking.

Zeke stood up, tapped his cigarette out, and went to work. He checked his rod and rummaged in his bait box for the gray slivers of slit up squid. Then he tugged the 400 watt out from his pack and set it on the railing. He spun the bolts to anchor it in place and swiveled it downward.

Harpooning off the sword boat was hard work. Pier fishing was easy. Pier fishing with a spotlight? Now that was a breeze. Once he'd turned it on, the fish would come swarming.

As he readied to cast, he was already wondering what he'd catch. He hoped there'd be some more flounder. He'd had a good run on them lately. Stupid animals. All it took was a little bait and a little bit of light and they couldn't help themselves.

"Come on baby, I want you to swim..."

Zeke froze.

Someone was singing, far too close to be from the shore.

He turned toward the beach, but the drunk seemed just as surprised, his migration halted as he stared off toward the water.

The voice had been a woman's.

It came from below.

Zeke leaned over the edge and saw her there just at the edges of the moonlight. Some naked chick splashing around in the bay beneath the pier. She'd sprayed herself in something greenish and glowing. Safety paint, he supposed. The glowing kind they used for fire exits. He found himself remembering one of the deep sea drags he'd run on the *Espada*, when they pulled up something that looked like a cross between a fish and a rotten watermelon, its mouth gaping stupidly, a softly glowing tendril on its tongue.

Zeke shook his head. Water had to be near fifty degrees. The hell was she thinking? Dumb cooze. If he were younger, the whole display might've been erotic. Now it seemed stupid as hell. It was dangerous.

Probably some college chick wasted on speed and God only knew what else.

"Girl, you're hot as fuck," the drunk on the beach called out. "But damn. That water looks cold as a penguin's ass. No way am I going for a swim."

"Come and swim," she insisted again, a little hum following.

C'mon and Swim. That's what she was singing, he realized. The words weren't quite right, but he knew the tune. Hadn't heard that one since the '60s. Bobby Freeman and that stupid dance song. He hummed along for a moment before he could stop himself.

What kind of college girl sang songs from the 1960s?

He licked dry lips, spat out his cigarette and reached for a new one. His hand shook as he pulled one from the pack, but he didn't call out. He wasn't sure why the whole scene made him nervous, but it did.

The young man on the beach sighed and drunkenly fumbled at his belt.

"At least come a bit closer to shore. You're a whole mood, aren't you? Christ it's goddamn cold," he muttered as the water hit his ankles.

"Baby," she said. Her voice climbed in excitement. *"Come and swim ..."*

The girl drifted closer to shore. Not swam. Drifted. Like she was waist deep and floating, no matter the depth. Like she was a ghost. He shivered. His bladder felt tight and the fun of seeing some weird tryst lost all flavor of interest.

That wasn't how people moved and the glowing wasn't something just splashed on her. It was flickering, dancing along her as if it were alive. Maybe, he decided, he wouldn't turn the light on at all. Maybe he would just let them have their moment, drink his beer and head home. Keep his eyes to himself and his mouth shut. He didn't need fish tonight.

The drunk sloshed along through the slight swells and valleys while the girl hovered in wait, just out of reach, her body tensed and ready to spring.

But it wasn't a girl. Zeke knew that in his heart. Not a girl at all. He knew what it really was. The Hobbomock. Ol' Chepa.

He was more than just nervous, he realized. He was piss-the-bed scared. His hands were throbbing and he forced them to unclench. He needed to do something. Anything, really, that might keep the Hobbomock away from the poor drunken idiot.

But if he did… he could feel a memory of Foreman's filthy fingers trace down his spine, across his hips and lower. The cigarette slipped out from his loose lips, hit the deck and bounced. He didn't dare bend down to retrieve it. He couldn't look away. He couldn't catch his breath enough to call out.

The shadowy shapes met and the two became one.

The spotlight, he realized.

He gripped it, aimed it toward them and flipped the switch.

The light blazed down.

Zeke screamed.

CHAPTER FIVE:

Eric woke up to the flicker of flashing reds and blues creeping in through the slats in the blinds along with the morning sunlight. The lights cut off and a moment later, a police officer was pounding at the door. Police had a way of knocking that seemed wholly different.

The sound took him immediately back to the night his father had been arrested.

The chirrup of sirens, the blazing fireworks of light, the fist battering the door. How he'd stumbled out of his room in time to see his father in handcuffs as two men in uniform escorted him toward one of the cruisers parked out front. The outraged confusion as his mother demanded to know what they were doing. How they dared put the sheriff in handcuffs. Why no one would explain to her what was going on.

His father had remained silent, head bowed in submission.

That night Eric had been desperate to know more, for someone to talk to him, to tell what was happening, to offer any sort of comfort—although no one did any of those.

Now, Eric laid on his back among a tangle of sweaty sheets and stared up at the ceiling. The sun on the far side of the blinds threw a glowing ladder across his bed and he fumbled for his phone. No text messages, of course. First period was already well underway.

The front door swung open, and he could picture his mother standing there, still in her Orinco Gas polo, as she stared down whoever had come to call.

"Keep those fucking lights off when you come here," she said.

"Jenny, can I come in?

Mr. Marty's voice. His father's old partner.

"Fuck you," she said.

The man let out an audible sigh. His boots thudded on the hardwood as he headed in toward the kitchen where he stopped.

"Is Eric here?"

"Is it about Jack?"

"Naw, this is about… believe it or not, it's about a ten fifty-seven."

"Missing person?"

"Mhm. Possibly a killing, but hard to say."

"What do you want with me?"

"Actually, I wanted to talk to Eric." Silence stretched for a long moment before Mr. Marty's continued. "Don't worry, it's not like that. He didn't do anything."

"I know he didn't. He's asleep. He can't help you."

"Jenny, it's a school day. I just need to talk to him for a minute, then I'll drive him in myself, save him the bike ride. If I get another truancy report…"

"He can't help you. And don't call me that. Not anymore."

"Ma'am."

Eric returned to looking up at the ceiling, following cracks which arched like gray lightning through the plaster. He wondered what it would feel like if the whole roof just plummeted down.

Ma'am.

That was the strangest part.

Mr. Marty was an inextricable part of Eric's childhood. Eric had sat across from his sister as Mr. Marty and their dad showed them both how to play Spades and Hearts, how to shuffle cards and palm off aces. They were both Coleridge sheriffs, but Mr. Marty wasn't just his father's coworker. He may as well have been one of the Rosses. They'd all eaten lobsters together on the porch as the sun eased into the forested horizon, fingers gliding over the bony armor, their wrists greasy from melted butter. Mr. Marty was family, had always been family.

Eric even had some hazy recollection of sneaking out long past his bedtime and seeing his mother kissing the man in the entryway to their house, her face flushed as she leaned up and brushed his lips with her own. How he had laughed and told her goodnight while his father snored on the sofa.

He'd never told anyone, of course. He wasn't even certain if the memory was real or a fabrication. Not that it mattered in the long run anyway.

"He won't help you, you know. Not after what you did to Jack."

The man cleared his throat.

"I didn't—Jack committed murder."

"It was defense and you know it. That boy was trying to take our daughter from us."

He sighed again.

"Tiffany was seventeen years old. Not the first time a father didn't like his girl's boyfriend."

"He hit her."

"Jenny, that *boy* wasn't fighting back. He just stood there, and Jack cut him down at a bus station. A dozen witnesses. You've read the police report. Your own daughter's testimony. Look, I'm not here about Jack. Hear me out. Some asshole was out fishing on the Bay Point after hours. Broke in, whatever. Anyway, he told me he saw someone out in the water. Some naked woman or something. He said she killed my missing person. Ripped his face right off. Bad enough that the fisher is holed up in a psych ward over at Southcoast."

Eric felt as if he'd been punched in the gut.

He sat up, turned toward the door to listen more closely.

They couldn't be talking about her. It wasn't possible, was it? It had to be some other naked woman out in the water. Some naked woman… or something.

The feeling of vague, predatory menace echoed back from the night before. The claws. The teeth. His heart beat drummed in his ears. They couldn't take her away, too. He'd just met her. It wasn't fair.

Just some drunk's accusation. She was *his* secret, not theirs. And besides, R'hial *liked* him. He had to give her the benefit of the doubt.

"Marty, I don't know what angle you're trying to work, but we're done here."

"I'm only asking because I know your boy spends a lot of time out on the pier. Maybe he saw something."

"Keeping tabs?"

"Maybe I am checking in on Jack's kid. Is that so bad? I'm looking after him, Jenny. I'm trying to. God only knows what you're on. Pills? Drunk? This place is a shitshow. You can barely sit upright. It's half past eight on a Monday morning and your kid is still sleeping. He should already be at school. Jesus Christ. I'm trying to save a life here."

An awful, heavy silence answered him.

"You know what prison is like for police, Marty? He was your partner."

The hate in her voice made Eric shiver.

"Jenny—"

"No. You don't say my name in my house. Get out."

"I miss Jack too."

"I said, 'Get out.'"

"Ma'am."

The chair slid back. The floor creaked as the man stood.

Eric kicked off his blankets and rushed out to catch him.

"Mr. Marty?" The man was halfway through the doorway, his wide-brimmed hat in hand and gun on his hip as he looked for some words to placate Eric's mother. The image of the two kissing reverberated for a moment before flickering away. "Mr. Marty, you said a naked woman was killing people?"

The sheriff studied him; his brow furrowed as he chewed his lower lip.

"Hey Eric, buddy. You know anything about her?"

His mother let out a sound similar to a growl from where she sat on the couch.

"Get back to your room, Eric. Don't tell him shit."

"Mom. I don't know anything, anyway. I was just curious."

Mr. Marty chewed on his lip, tucked his thumbs into his tool belt.

"Just curious?"

"About the naked woman in the water. Was there really a murder?"

Eric's mother slammed her fist down against the coffee table and the orange bottle toppled from its perch. Pills rattled as they skittered in every direction.

"You listen to me! This is my house!" She lurched to her feet and Eric felt a pang of embarrassment. Her hair was tangled in a dull rat's nest, her shirt miss-buttoned so peeks of pale skin were visible through cracks. Her eyes had half circles beneath them deep enough that she might as well have been in a fight. She bared her teeth at the two of them. "Marty, get out. Don't come in here without a warrant. Eric, go get ready for school."

Eric flinched.

Mr. Marty ignored her. "I don't know if there was a murder, but supposedly my missing person—college kid named Travis Mitchell—went out in the water by the Bay Point and didn't come back. Might've just gone for a swim, or… well… you tell me. The story the fisherman told was pretty wild, but we did find the kid's phone and some clothes that match his description. You seen anything out there, Eric? Anything pretty wild?"

Eric tried not to blink as he shook his head. He wasn't sure why he lied. Eric's mother pointed at the door.

"Out!"

Mr. Marty nodded to her, then to him.

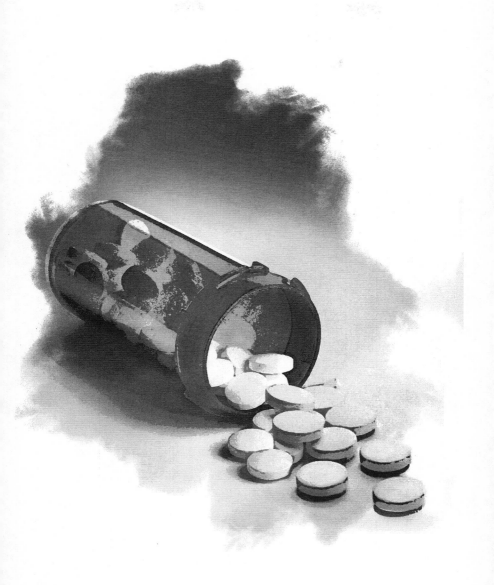

"Mrs. Ross. Eric."

He touched his hat one last time, and pulled the door closed behind him. His mother sank down onto the couch and began to sob. Eric fled to his room, suddenly dizzy.

In through your nose, out through your mouth.

It couldn't be her. She wouldn't have actually killed anyone. Would she?

He fumbled in his hamper for the least stained t shirt he could find—another of his dad's plain white undershirts that were two sizes too big and no longer really white—and changed into it. The rest of his clothes stayed the same from the day before. By the time he headed back out and grabbed a slice of bread from the bag, his mother was on her hands and knees, scooping at the pills and trying to put them back in the orange tube. Her medicine slipped between her fingers as her hands shook.

He grabbed his backpack.

She didn't look up when he said goodbye.

CHAPTER SIX:

Coleridge High, home of the Fighting Albatross, had turned strange.

Eric was never particularly popular in his class, even before the killing—Christian Yarrow had been his friend, and Sean Hargrove and Nick Roles were close enough that he would visit their house every now and then, but he was far from a social force. He'd just been one of the normal kids. Nothing special. Better grades than most and a knack for drawing, but nothing particularly noteworthy. His daydreams of standing out had just been idle fantasies.

After the murder, he got his wish. He'd stood out alright.

Coleridge was a small town, and the dead boy had been a student, just a semester away from graduating. His brother Brandon was only a year behind him. The community was more or less unified in its decision.

Christian abandoned him immediately. Told him to his face that he was done being his friend. The Yarrows lived in the same trailer park as the Anders and his allegiance was clear. Sean and

Nick hadn't said anything, but there were no more invites to their houses and after a few weeks they didn't even spare him a glance at lunch. Eric ended up eating standing, shoveling his food down next to the sour-smelling trashcan.

Now Eric hunched behind his desk at the back of the classroom, picking the edge scraps from his notebook's spiral binding. He'd filled the notebook up last year, but there was still a good amount of space on the back of the pages and in the margins.

Mrs. Grenada droned on in front of the white board, coaxing the class through a one-sided discussion of past participles. She had dark eyes, a lilting Hispanic accent and a bright enough smile that she almost made the class interesting. The curls of her hair always looked slightly damp, like she'd stepped out fresh from the shower.

He'd had a crush on her for years, spent more than one class fantasizing about running his fingers through her hair and over her skin. Awful, wonderful thoughts that set him flushed and unsteady and aching, although even in the privacy of his own mind he shied away from thinking too much about The Act that he'd read about, that he'd seen on his phone when the Wi-Fi wasn't stalling out. Mostly he just liked to picture sitting next to her on the Lover's Bench on the pier, fingers intertwined, her head on his shoulder. That was the thought that ached the most.

Some days he'd doodle pictures of the bench like it was their secret.

Today, he found himself drawing pictures of R'hial, instead.

The shading on her cheeks was all wrong and the nose could have been anyone's, but the odd shape of her eyes was right. The edge of her teeth peeking between her lips looked sharp enough to cut the paper. He was getting better, he realized. Still not good enough, he reminded himself. The face he'd drawn was pretty, but not yet beautiful.

Certainly not the face of a murderer, though.

Whatever Mr. Marty thought he knew, there was no way she would have hurt some guy. Unless she felt like she really had to, he supposed. Maybe he had threatened her, attacked her, something like that. For a moment, he wished he'd asked Mr. Marty for more details, but the feeling passed.

She was his secret. He didn't want to share.

The clock finished its revolution and the bell let out an ugly jangle. A moment later and students were spilling up and out of their seats as the principal's disembodied voice came over the intercom listing afterschool programs and whatever else. Eric didn't pay any attention. He studied the drawing instead.

He waited until the rest of the students had filed out, laughing and chatting, gliding across the surface of the day without a glance back toward him. When they were gone, he breathed a sigh of relief and stuffed the notebook into his backpack, one of the few things he owned that wasn't turning threadbare and frayed. A treasured relic from the year before, before all the legal fees and food stamps.

He'd made it halfway to the door when Ms. Grenada cleared her throat.

"Eric, do you have a moment?"

He froze mid step, a flush creeping up his neck. He thought of the Lover's Bench and then tried to think about anything else.

"Hey, Ms. Grenada."

Maude Grenada, the name plate on her desk announced from its perch among the neat, orderly stacks of papers. She did not look at all like a Maude.

"I wanted to talk with you. I tried to call your mother, but she wouldn't answer."

"What's up?"

She paused, steepled her fingers, and stared at the tips as if carefully measuring and balancing her words.

"I know things are hard at home and that you're going through a lot. I wish there was some way I could help. But Eric, I need something a little more to work with. You used to be an all-around A student. I've checked with your other teachers, now you're not even on course to pass. You can do this work, I know you can, but… and it's not just that, either. I don't mean to make you feel any kind of way, but you may want to clean up a bit. Your clothes. A shower, maybe…"

He stared at her.

She looked right back, a blush of her own creeping along her cheekbones, but even that was pretty and somehow it made him feel even worse. She bit her lower lip before continuing.

"Please, don't feel embarrassed. I know it's hard, but… well… there've been a few complaints, and between that and all the days you've been missing…"

He turned back toward the door, squeezed his eyes shut to keep the wet heat inside them. He wanted the conversation to stop. Anything to make her stop talking. He didn't want to cry, couldn't bear the thought of that humiliation on top of the rest.

"Okay," he whispered.

"I'm not trying to embarrass you. You're a good kid. I just want to help. I want to make sure that you don't get lost in this whole mess while we can still control—"

"Can I go?"

She sighed.

"Yes, Eric. You can go."

He wiped at his eyes and rushed out the door, down the hallway and into sunlight that yielded little warmth.

The other students had mostly already fled, so he went to his bike, fixed the habitually loose chain and cleared the lock. The gears were gritty from caked on salt and the steel frame had seen better days, but it didn't look cheap. It just looked well-traveled. The mud and the dents were proud. The flat tires... well, that part did look a bit cheap, but it still drove well enough.

He glanced up on a whim and he saw them a few moments before they noticed him.

Brandon, still dressed in his brother's leather jacket, the other two flanking him. Eric understood Christian being there, but he could never really figure out why anyone let Handsy on school property. He didn't go to Coleridge High, didn't go to school anywhere at all as far as Eric knew, but he was generally known to be a nice, not-too-bright kid, so no one ever called him out. Brandon was taller and bigger than any of them, but Eric couldn't help but view him with a little bit of contempt. Eric's father had arrested Brandon's for a DUI a few years back, after he crashed his car heading back from a bar to the trailer park off Pleasant Oak where their whole clan lived. When Tiffany started dating Brandon's brother, he'd seen the look of disgust on his father's face and adopted it for himself.

Trailer trash.

And then a few months later, his father had shot him.

Brandon's head was on a swivel. Looking for him, Eric decided. They hadn't caught up with him in the last week or so and that meant that it was overdue. Not that Christian or the other boy seemed very enthusiastic about the hunt, but they weren't ones to dissuade their friend.

Eric didn't wait. He kicked his bike free of the stand and took off, his legs straining, the tires letting out their flat, flatulent grind as he rumbled along.

By the time Brandon called out his name it was too late and the taller boy simply stared after him, fading into the landscape as Eric made his getaway.

CHAPTER SEVEN:

He didn't head home.

The thought of retreating to that shell of a life, with its stale bread and yellowed milk, the smell of filthy dishwater and decay, all to wallow in the shame of Ms. Grenada's gentle reminder—*maybe a shower?*—was just too much.

He headed to the pier.

Two miles later, he re-set his bike's chain and locked it, then made his way down the stairs.

The sun was still up, but the shadows cast by the cliff face enveloped most of the beach and kept the sand and pebbles in a premature twilight. The chill remained.

He kicked his way across the beach, trying his best to not let himself think about why he'd come. The tarp had been disturbed but the tepid pools of spray and grit were again home to buzzing gnats. A tattered flag of police tape fluttered like a finish line ribbon from the first of the pilings to a cheap wooden stake planted beside the staircase, although not much effort had been used to secure it and Eric ducked under without difficulty. The ocean made for a pretty poor crime scene.

If there had even been a crime.

Just a year ago, the idea of murder had seemed an impossibility. A mechanism for court room television and dull movies with too much talking. A lot had changed since then, but did he really believe some drunk who claimed his mermaid had killed someone?

His mermaid.

An electric sort of anxiety pumped through him, a sensation he didn't quite understand but one that he never wanted to let go.

She wouldn't come back, he told himself. Whatever he thought he had found the night before, that all had to be some sort of trick. He should head back up the stairs, get his bike and go home. That's what common sense said to do.

Entering between the pilings felt like lowering himself into a cave. The wooden columns on either side choked off most of the sunlight, shadowed the water to the point of opaque blackened ripples. The stench of the wood hung heavy in the air, the arsenic-infused pine still carrying a yellow gasoline-like reek even after all their sea-swept years. Above, the pier gave the impression of a timid reach out toward the ocean, a half-hearted entreaty toward the wider sea. Underneath, it felt like an endless tunnel. The distant, choked star of light at the far end only increased the subterranean impression.

Not just a cave.

A tomb.

Someone had died there, just hours before.

Doubting had been easier in the sunlight.

The wood creaked under the weight of the burden they held above him, sea foam hissed susurrating whispers against the pilings.

Barnacles pitted the wood with jagged acne scars, their glistening bony bodies like the sunken nubs of teeth, their centers like tiny wet eyes.

Eric shivered, tried to focus on the light instead.

Why did he even want her to come back? She had *killed* someone.

Hadn't she?

The light at the end of the tunnel grew stronger, shifted.

First the soft glow of her hair beneath the gray, that splash of greenish luminescence, then her forehead breached beside one of the deeper pillars. Long-nailed fingers gripped the wood and lifted her face just high enough that those strange, dark eyes found him. A glitter of alien radiance sparkled in their depths like distant stars as she studied him. He raised a hand in greeting.

"Hey," he said. He wished he knew some better way to start a conversation.

She dipped under and when she resurfaced she had slipped closer, crossed from pillar to pillar and neared the shore. The crest of scales glinted behind her in the water as she moved, a serpentine train gliding through the froth and murk.

She raised a hand in greeting, tilting it from side to side. The flat blade of her fingernails made him think of his father's pocket knife. At what point, he wondered, were nails considered claws?

"Justaric," she said.

A spider-legged rush of nervousness crawled across his skin.

"Hi, R'hial."

He hoped he had the pronunciation correct.

"Come on and swim?"

He couldn't quite make out her face among the shadows. The flickering glow illuminating only the intensity of her gaze, but he could feel the importance of the question. He shook his head and licked his lips before he responded.

"The police are looking for you."

"Police?" She hummed for a moment. "Stand so close to meee…"

"Huh? No, like, someone saw you. They said you killed someone last night."

She flinched.

"I…"

"It's okay. No one believes him. No one will find out that you're here. I won't… I won't tell."

"I—R'Scylla said I bring but I—but not right—"

Her words tumbled out in a panicked, incomprehensible rush. Eric shook his head.

"It doesn't matter. I don't care why you did it."

She remained hunched against the piling, each slow rolling crest reaching to her chin, each valley baring down to her pale shoulder. She shook her head in mute frustration.

"My dad killed someone too," he said. "It's okay."

With his eyes better adjusted it was easier to pick out her expression, if not to understand it. She looked almost sad.

"Have you?" she asked. "Killing?"

"No."

He felt, oddly, ashamed.

Have you considered taking a shower? Killing?

"Only eat popcorn? Dogcorn?"

"I've eaten meat. Animals, I mean."

"Not killing?"

"Other people did the killing. I just ate the meat. I could though, I mean." He thought of Brandon. "I could kill. If I needed to. Is that... is that why you killed him? For food?"

She studied him for a long moment.

"No," she whispered.

She turned and looked off into the ocean behind her. He wished he hadn't said anything about the police. If she left now, there wouldn't be any reason for her to come back. He'd be alone again. Alone. He tried to smother the rush of panic that flitted into his mind like television static.

"Please don't go. Not yet."

He remembered the desperate, hungry way she had watched his feet before and he kicked off his shoes, peeled off browning socks and tossed them in a heap beside the buggy tarp. He wiggled his toes as the wet cold sucked up into him from the ground. It felt like standing on frozen iron.

"Here. See?"

She hesitated and then drifted closer to stare at them.

"Come on and swim?" she asked, but with none of her previous enthusiasm. She shook her head.

"How about I bring you something. Tomorrow. A gift."

"A gift," she said.

"If you come back again."

"Again."

She leaned against one of the half-pilings, her fingers scraping lazy circles over the bent, metal cap. The sound made his skin ache. A tiny translucent crab scuttled out from a hidden vantage point beneath the beaten metal and made a break for it. One of R'hial's nails impaled it. The legs wobbled, continued their crawling motion as she examined it and the syrupy ooze that streamed from its broken body. Then she plucked it off her nail with her mouth. Each chew let out a wet crunch.

Eric fought a sudden urge to vomit.

"Does it taste good?" he asked.

"Does popcorn?"

Far out past the breakers, he heard the distant sound again. Barely a rumble, but one that found a home deep inside his gut. He wondered if he would have even noticed it, if he weren't standing with his feet in the surf beneath the pier's wooden funnel.

R'hial startled, turned and slithered back deeper into the water.

"What is that? The sound."

She hesitated.

"My father also kills," she said, as if it were an explanation. Eric supposed it was. "Again?"

"Again," he said.

And then she was gone.

CHAPTER EIGHT:

Eric stayed home on Tuesday.

Tiff called on Tuesdays, so instead of climbing onto his bike and haunting the back of the Coleridge High classrooms, he spent the morning sitting at the kitchen table across from his mother. She had a standing excuse with the school, or so she said. Eric didn't question it. The old landline phone sat on the table between them, a religious offering laid out to appease some higher power. On the far side of the table, the two empty chairs stood witness.

There was no real schedule for when Tiffany would contact them. Sometimes the call came early. Sometimes Eric would have to wait for hours. This one was from the second group.

The sun rose and the morning passed with his mother drumming her fingers on the wood and him wishing he could find a comfortable position in his chair. He felt like he was back in the courtroom, sitting in the row of wooden benches so like the pews of a church, waiting for that final verdict. Not that there had been any doubt. No deal had been offered.

When it had come, his father had turned to him, leaned over the barrier, and gripped Eric's shoulder. His breath had smelled like cigarettes. His hands had trembled, but there were no tears in his eyes.

"You're the man now," he'd said. *"You'll be okay. You can make it. Strong like Armystrong. You'll be fine."*

Eric's mom had put them to bed with stories of Winnie the Pooh. Eric's dad had told them Army stories. Stories about insurmountable odds, stories with names like Sudan and Somalia. Men killing and men dying. Saving and surrendering. Convoys trapped on roadsides. Ranger companies marching the Mogadishu Mile through a city bent on killing them. That was real strength, he said. Being able to put blood in the sand and still finding your way home. That was real toughness.

Eric wondered if it was any tougher than watching his father walk the two dozen feet from the court room, cuffed and gripped by two grim-faced sheriffs, the prisoner of a pointless struggle. Tiffany never came back from Boston, not even for her boyfriend's funeral or her father's arraignment.

Eric wondered whether it was any tougher than sitting at the table across from his hollow-eyed mother, strands of hair trapped in her mouth and tangled into wispy sailing knots as she stared down the phone.

"She'll call, won't she?"

"Sure will, mom."

Eric wasn't sure why his sister still called. Maybe his mom had some sort of deal worked out with her or maybe it was a simple, irrational pattern, but he had come to dread it. They'd been close, once,

Tiff and him. Before the constant arguing, the increasingly early curfews, the sneaking out and the drinking and the threats. Back before she could only talk about the day that she'd catch the Greyhound out of New Bedford and never come back. A simpler time.

He missed her, but every Tuesday he spent the day wishing she would stop calling altogether.

The phone rang and his mother grabbed it up on the first ring. She dabbed at her eyes with the back of her wrist, her mouth working into an imitation of a smile so that she could force the emotion past her lips.

"Hey there, honey!"

The two chattered for a moment, the unnatural cheeriness grating on Eric's nerves. Nothing important was said, from what he could tell. Weather. Work. Eric's mom tilted her head and nodded along. Her fingers did not stop drumming on the tabletop.

He could only hear part of the conversation, but he filled in the gaps and pieced enough together to follow along. His mother's face held a hundred questions she never dared ask, pieces missing too, until all that was left was a dance of pointless pleasantries. Anything to avoid the heart of it. Anywhere but home. He wondered if Tiffany held just as much back.

Eric's mom gave in first.

"I miss you," she said, at last. The tiny voice on the far line had been rambling, something about the coming winter, but it cracked and faltered at the intrusion. Eric imagined it was partly relief. The rules had been broken. The conversation was over, the same as every Tuesday. Someone had to blink first for the staring contest to end. Eric's mother continued, "Do you think...?"

Her fingers turned pale as they squeezed the phone to death. Her rictus faltered, her jaw clenching until the individual cords of muscle stood out.

Tiffany said something that Eric couldn't make out. His mom closed her eyes, nostrils flared.

"I get it. I definitely do. Work is crazy here, too. I know you're—okay. Okay. Do you want to talk to Er-bear?" Her shoulders slumped. "Okay. Okay. Next Tuesday? Tiff, honey, I love you."

Eric's fingernails dug into his palms, but he tried his best to keep the sting of it from his face. Not even a hello. His mother waited a moment longer, but Eric couldn't hear if Tiffany said it back, and then she set the phone on the table in front of her. The smile slid off her face and she seemed to transform in front of him, to reduce, to crumble away.

He reached across the pile of mail and took her hand in his own. She still had not opened her eyes.

"I miss him," she said at last. "I miss them both. There's nothing like it. This whole place... We need to get out of this shithole. Pack up and just... go."

Her language had always been pristine, before. The words sounded strangely natural, though, and Eric wondered if she's been cursing for years, hiding her habit like Sean Hargrove's dad tried to hide that he still smoked weed.

"Sure mom."

"Tomorrow. Maybe tomorrow. We get in the car and go." She paused "You know what I told him before he did it? I told him to keep our Tiffany safe."

She shook her head.

"Mom…"

He glanced at the clock that hung on the wall.

School would let out soon. The pier would open and *she* would be waiting beneath it. Waiting for *him*, and not refusing to speak to him on the phone. His mother continued.

"And I can't even… Things just fall apart so quickly. I wish—" she seemed to realize who she was talking to and pull herself together. "We never ate lunch. I'll make mac and cheese, I think there's some pepperoni, yeah? Your favorite."

It had been, once. When Eric was six.

"Sure mom. Sounds great. I was thinking in a little bit that I could go grab dinner at the pier?"

Not that there was money for it, of course, but he could usually sneak a few handfuls of popcorn from the side of the cart before anyone got irritated.

She frowned at him.

"You spend too much time there."

"Mom…"

"I guess you can. Wear your jacket, though. Or you could stay home and we can watch a movie with me? It'll be just like old times. Won't be long before you get yourself a girl and then you'll be gone and it'll just be me knocking around here."

She nodded toward the couch.

Eric hesitated. The couch was filthy, stained, smelled like body odor and a little like urine. Like his mother. He wondered what Mrs. Grenada would say about her, and the thought made him suddenly, powerfully sad. He understood Tiffany's betrayal, but it hurt just the same.

"Sure mom," he said.

Once they'd eaten, he sat down on the stinking sofa beside her and slipped into the television's dull glow. He wondered what R'hial was doing. As the day marched on toward night, he found his eyes drifting back up to the clock on the wall.

When he spared a glance for his mom, he found her eyes drifting back down to the orange bottle.

CHAPTER NINE:

Wednesday crawled along at a glacial pace and Eric shambled from class to class, waiting for the final bell to ring and set him free. His drawings were getting better. Not just her face, but her body, down to her tail with its diaphanous trimming of fins. Still a work in progress, but a few hours of practice had helped a lot.

He wondered whether R'hial was floating out among the waves, waiting for the pier to come to life. Was she waiting for him? Had she gone home? Did she even have a home? He allowed himself to imagine a hidden Atlantis kingdom, crested with golden towers and glowing battlements, bustling with life. He realized he hadn't asked her that. He should have asked her that.

Thinking about her made the day bearable. He was going to see her in a few hours, then in a few minutes, then he was just waiting for the bell. Even Mrs. Grenada's worried looks deflected off him without much pain. She passed back a quiz to the other kids, but he didn't recall taking one and she had none for him. He had a hard time caring about that either. He'd missed a bunch before. Nothing new.

71

He wondered if R'hial took tests too.

He'd brought gifts for her from home, packed his backpack full of whatever he could find around the house that she might not recognize. Things that might excite her. A ball of yarn, silverware, a small collection of rocks in a plastic, segmented case. A stack of National Geographic magazines, their bright yellow borders faded and bent from use. Even if she couldn't take them with her, they could share them together for a few minutes, side by side. And to make up for missing her on Tuesday, he'd brought a special gift, lent to him by his father before all the mess. He tried not to think too hard about it, as if one of his classmates would be able to read his ugly secret on his face. No one could know he'd brought that to school. It would all be worth it soon enough.

A bike ride away. That was all it took.

When the bell rang and the voice on the intercom finished, he hitched up his backpack. He realized he was smiling as he walked—jogged, really—toward the bike rack.

He was so caught up in his wanting that he didn't feel them closing in until Brandon gripped the backpack and jerked it off his shoulders. He went down in a heap, knees and elbows banging against the sidewalk.

"The fuck you off to, killer?"

Brandon Anders stood over him, a look of disgust on his face. Christian and the Norwegian kid hung back, as they usually did. They were happy enough to support their friend but it was his show and neither of them seemed to have any real interest in getting dragged into the feud directly.

Eric climbed back to his feet and wiped his hands on his sweat-pants, tried to ignore the stinging red lines across his palms. Other students walked by, cast sidelong glances, but no one helped him. Of course they wouldn't. If anyone joined, they wouldn't be on his side. Brandon held the bag toward him, let it sway like a pendulum. When Eric reached to take it, the older boy tugged it just out of reach.

"Come on, Brandon. Give it back."

"I'm tired of you ducking me. What the hell you got in here anyway?"

Eric pictured them rummaging through his collection and he swallowed back a lump in his throat. He lunged for the backpack. Brandon jerked it away at the last moment and Eric's fingers barely caught the strap. He twisted the strap around his hand for leverage and threw himself backwards. The older boy bared his teeth, the struggle encouraging some inner ferocity.

The two hung in balance, feet planted and bodies bent away from each other.

Eric felt a sudden looseness and thought, for a moment, that he was winning. Then he was stumbling, the backpack yawning open like a frayed, broken jaw. The zipper dangled, a loose tooth waiting to drop, but for a moment he still thought that everything might somehow stay inside. Brandon gave it one final shake and it slipped out of Eric's hands.

His notebooks hit the ground and coughed out their secrets, scattered pages of artwork among the rattle of plastic and metal, pens, flapping magazines and rocks and yarn. Brandon shook it empty, then tossed the torn remains of the backpack to the side.

A hollowness opened in Eric's stomach as he realized *it* had fallen too.

Panic wired through him as he scanned through the wreckage.

Brendan crouched down and picked up one of the notebook's pages.

"A fucking *mermaid*? You some kind of fag?"

Christian let out a bark of laughter and Handsy made some comment or another, but Eric ignored them, his heartbeat thundering in his ears. His eyes darted from item to item until he saw the lacquered wooden handle and the glint of ugly metal along its edge. He scurried forward and grabbed it. His father's knife. Not some little Swiss Army knife. A real fold-out with a blade like a straight razor.

The backpack lay next to it, torn and wrung out. Ruined. One of the last possessions he had that wasn't at least on the brink of decay, one of the few remaining relics from before everything went to hell.

The others were so caught up in their mockery that they didn't look over until the blade clicked into place. Eric pressed it flat against his thigh. He wanted to hold it out toward them like some holy relic against evil, but there were other students. There were teachers. Everything seemed to slow down. His hands shook as they turned toward him, one by one.

A part of him realized he was crossing a line, a dangerous divide, and that certain decisions couldn't be unmade. He squeezed the grip until his fingers went numb.

"Well, holy shit. Little fag's got a knife."

Any humor had left Brandon's voice.

"Jesus," Christian said. He held up his hands in surrender. "Dude."

"I ain't getting cut up for this shit," Handsy confided. He took a step back, then another. "You're crazy, kid."

Brandon didn't back down.

"What the fuck, Ross?"

The knife trembled, the tip of it digging into his leg.

"Get away from me or I'll… I'll…"

Eric tried to imagine using the knife on the taller boy, but his mind skittered away from the thought. Everything felt underwater. His vision darkened around the edges. A roaring filled his ears. He hoped he wasn't going to pass out.

Brandon studied the weapon in Eric's hands for a long moment. Then he stood and tore the picture of the mermaid in half without once looking away. The pieces of paper fluttered and skipped along in the breeze.

"Or you'll what? Gonna try and stab me? Well. Come on, then."

Eric's heart pounded. He dropped to one knee, grabbed a handful of the gifts and shoved them in his pocket. He didn't bother with the notebooks. He could always take some of Tiffany's old ones, once he got home.

"Just leave me alone," he whispered, when he could form the words.

He unlocked his bike—mercifully on the first try—and climbed onto it.

He fled.

CHAPTER TEN:

The beach was empty.

Eric waited in the fitful cold, feeling like an idiot, staring out at the nothing for a half hour. Icy spray leapt and spat against the pilings, the froth the color of bone in the darkness.

Had he really thought she would be there for him? That she would feel any of what he felt? He wanted to scream his frustration out. To throw something or stab something. He thought of Brandon and the others and wished, for a moment, that they'd tried to grab him. That he'd gotten to at least make someone else bleed for once instead of just one more humiliation. One more betrayal, one more piece of life twisting against him. Like that story he'd read in grade school, about the person who turned everything to gold by touching it. Except he transformed things into shit.

He was just about ready to give up and slink on back home when she surfaced only a handful of paces away. No gentle approach this time, just an appearance as if out of nothing, her head sliding out among the push and pull of cloudy water. He was amazed at how close she got to the shore without him noticing.

"R'hial! Hey there," he said. He waved to her but she did not return the gesture.

"You came back."

"Of course I came back."

She leaned back into the water, only her face bobbing above the rolling surface and the shadows of her breasts just beneath. As if she were the face of the ocean itself.

"Not yesterday."

"I was busy."

"I waited."

He scratched at his matted hair, his excitement fading by the moment. She looked up into the cloud riddled sky, not at him. Her nails flexed and cut momentary furrows in the water.

"I'm sorry. I didn't know. I had stuff I had to do. I'll always be back though, okay? Mom always says we'll leave but we're never gonna. I'll always be here. The pier has always been here. None of us are going anywhere."

She continued her lazy, sinuous path for a moment more before resting a hand on one of the rotted columns from some ancient pier that had stood and fallen long before the Bay Point. She traced a finger over the pitted, shriveled remnants. Her body bobbed up and down with the shift of the sand-thickened waves.

"No," she said. "Not always."

"You won't be here?"

"You won't. The pier won't." She frowned. "Before was only sand. Sand and waves and stone. No pier. No music. One day..."

He squinted up at the wooden bridge hovering overhead like some sort of alien construct. The pier had been around since some time in the sixties, from what he'd heard, although he had a hard time really grasping how long ago that was. That meant it was even older than his parents. Mr. Yarrow's father had opened it. That meant it was *old*. And before that had been other, smaller piers for fishing boats to anchor. He'd seen pictures in the town hall when they visited on a field trip. The pictures had been washed out, sepia toned into timeless dustiness; photographs of oilskin-clad captains trudging through hurricane winds, the triangular peaks of old churches and the rocky cliffs, but never an image of the Coleridge beach without some sort of pier visible.

"How old are you?" He asked. "Sorry. I'm not supposed to ask girls that. Women, I mean."

She faced him at last, unsmiling.

"Take off shoes," she said. He did. "Talk the pier. Now. Slowly."

She hummed a snatch of the boardwalk song from above, but the notes were hurried, frustration plain on her face.

"Oh, uh, you know. Same as usual. Lights, music. Food, rides, people. They won't have it running for too many more weeks. The pier will still be open, but it's too cold for the rides during the winter, so Mr. Yarrow keeps them off. He's the guy in charge up there." He realized he was babbling and cut himself off. "What's it like where you live?"

She was silent for a while.

He tried to resummon the mental image he'd had before of shining walls and gilded buttresses, but he knew it was a lie even before she answered.

"No music. No light. Always cold."

Not some sprawling golden kingdom. Of course not. Just one more empire of darkness. He wanted to ask if she had friends like her, but he was afraid of the answer.

She continued staring at his feet.

"Do you like ice cream?"

"You scream?"

"Ice. And then cream. I don't have one this time. It's a kind of cold food made from milk and sugar. It's delicious."

She wrinkled her nose.

"Like popcorn?"

"It's different. I don't have any today. I do have a few things you might like though. Things you might not know. Gifts. From…" he gestured up the stairs behind him.

He fought a primal urge to run, to crawl, to scurry away from her. Instead he waited until the water pulled back and then darted forward, jumped and scrambled up out onto the metal capped piling from before, just far enough out into the water that he could have almost reached out and touched her if he dared. He flinched as the spray flung its icy spit against his bare ankles.

R'hial watched, eyes luminous, as he rummaged in his pocket and pulled the handful of treasures he'd managed to salvage from his ruined backpack. He leaned down and set the objects out one by one on a wooden post that she could easily reach.

"Here," he said.

"A fork?"

"Yeah, I thought that maybe you didn't…"

She raised an eyebrow and a slow smile spread across her face. She nodded her head toward the small drift of trash at the base of the stairs—Styrofoam cups, straws and plastic silverware, all crammed between the rocks.

"I know forks, Eric. And spoons."

Eric wished he'd saved the yarn instead. He set the spork out next.

"What about this one?"

She stared at it.

"What."

"It's a spork. It can be a spoon or a fork."

She picked it up carefully, probed it with her fingers, then clutched it to her chest.

"Mine," she said. Her voice took on a pleading edge. "Mine. Now."

"Yeah. Sure. It probably floats, though. You'll need to..." he shrugged. He had no idea what she wanted to do with it, so he didn't bother explaining. He took the knife out from his pocket next. He considered unfolding the blade, but realized he didn't want her to think he was doing anything dangerous.

Some neglected, wiser part of him noted that he already was doing something dangerous. That maybe he should keep the knife in hand, and ready.

He held it out to her.

"I had some magazines, too—books with pictures. But..."

She accepted the prized knife without comment or much interest, then returned her attention to the spork.

"Open it," he urged. "But be careful, it's sharp. Danger."

He expected her to fumble to extricate the blade but she flicked it open without pause. She tilted the blade and stared at herself in the reflection. Rocked it side to side to study herself. She didn't speak for a long while. She did not let go of the spork. Finally, she nodded. "More?"

"That's all. I don't have much today, sorry. They broke my backpack."

"Backpack?" she asked. "They?"

The sound, far out among the waves cut him off before he thought of a way to explain Brandon to her. Time was up.

"It's early today."

"Bring more gifts," she said. "Tomorrow."

"Tomorrow. You could stay a little longer, if you want? Whatever that is, it can wait. I missed you."

"No wait, Eric. Again. Spork."

She flicked the knife closed and set it on the metal beside him. He reached out to grab it and her hand shot out and gripped his wrist. Her palm was cold and slick and he was suddenly and intensely aware of her nakedness. Of her closeness. Of her teeth. She smelled of salt and something not altogether pleasant. Her claws were like steel against his skin. He tried to jerk his hand back, but she only smiled and squeezed tighter.

A sudden burst of panic rose up in his chest.

She was strong, he realized, far stronger than he expected for her slim frame. Strong enough that the bones in his wrist ached, that he couldn't help but think of the torn backpack and how easily it had all come apart. He wondered if he could pull away from her if he tried, or if he would lose some vast game of tug-of-war and end up dragged out among the waves and the endless dark. His fingers fumbled over the knife's handle, but he doubted it would do much good even if he could somehow get the blade out.

A second roll of the sound, louder this time.

"No wait again," she said.

"I'll be here," he said. "Tomorrow."

She nodded and released him. Before he could think of what else to say, she turned and with a flash of emerald scales she cut back into the water and shot like an arrow away from the shore.

CHAPTER ELEVEN:

r. Yarrow was waiting for him up by the bike rack, his thumbs tucked under suspender straps as he chewed a mouthful of tobacco.

"Was wondering when you'd be back." He nodded at the Schwinn. "Got a moment?"

Eric tried to keep the guilt from his face. Did Yarrow know about her? He glanced toward the stairs. They'd been half under the pier, but if he had leaned over to look...

If Yarrow had seen R'hial, he gave no hint of it.

"What's up?"

"Walk and talk. Gotta close this show up for the night."

Eric followed behind the big man as he led the way past the ticket booths, through the front gates and out onto the pier. Mr. Yarrow's voice boomed above the music as they went.

"I'm calling it early. No money in late nights on weekdays, and it's too damn cold. No point in staying open for business if business is shit."

The radio kept on howling out its top forty pop songs, the same as it had every night that Eric could remember. He wondered if it had been playing them since the sixties.

Songs are easiest. Songs make everything groooovy.

Yarrow continued.

"That's the tricky part. Business. Rest is easy. Gloria—Christian's mom—she works that side. Hiring, schedules. I do the fun stuff. Always had a knack for fixing shit. How old are you?"

"Fourteen."

He shrugged.

"For fixing *stuff*," he reiterated. "A little upkeep goes a long way. You get a feel for when the rides are up gonna fuck up. Sixth sense or something."

Eric waited for him to elaborate, but the man kept walking. He led the way past the Lover's Bench and over to the carousel's control podium, kicked the block out from the pedal and twisted the key out. The grind of turning gears immediately died. He hung the key on a hook beneath the controls and headed past the lines of impaled animals. When he got to the mirror-paneled center he gripped it and pulled open a hidden hatch of a door. Eric watched, fascinated. Yarrow clicked his pocket flashlight on and tucked the tail end in his mouth as he leaned in. A dull clack echoed through the night as he hit the breakers and killed the power to the speakers, to the radio, to the constant reel of music.

Only the lights remained, clustered like stars against the night sky.

He wondered if she was still out there, near enough that she could hear the music die out for the night. He ran his hand over the wrought iron back of the Lover's Bench. For all he'd daydreamed about it, he'd never touched it before. It was always occupied or he was too embarrassed to, with the other teens strolling by to see him.

Mr. Yarrow tucked the flashlight back in his pocket and a wad of chewing tobacco into his cheek.

"The damn thing is just a bench, you know," he said. "You need a girl."

"So… do you need me to help check the rides…?"

Mr. Yarrow snorted.

"No. God no. You're fourteen. End up killing everyone. I'd be out of business."

Eric thought again of R'hial's hand on his wrist. The forest of teeth and the strange hungry look on her face. He wondered how old she was, really. His dad had warned him about strange old men who might want to touch him, but it was different with her. Wasn't it?

"Mr. Yarrow, why…?"

"Why did I ask you out here?"

Eric nodded.

Mr. Yarrow chewed again and leaned over the railing to spit.

"Because the ride is about to fuck up. With you and those boys. Brandon's crew. Whatever happened with you at school today had Christian shook. And he wasn't worried for himself. Or for Brandon. He was worried for you. I know you two used to be friends, and he's scared for you. Look, it ain't my business, but don't mess with those boys."

The thought of Christian worrying about him brought an unexpected sting and Eric reminded himself of all those daily betrayals until the feeling fled.

"They shouldn't mess with me."

Yarrow nodded, chewed for a moment, then spat again, down into the waves.

"That's a numbers game, son. Only one of you. Know you miss your daddy, but that Anders boy misses his brother a whole lot worse. He can't send him letters or visit him on weekends. He's having a rough go of it."

Eric shrugged shoulders that should have carried his backpack. "Good."

The big man shook his head, his beard trailing behind the motion like an afterthought.

"Way he thinks of it, might as well have been you that killed his brother. Don't get me wrong, Sheriff was right. That boy had it coming. Any boy hurts one of my daughters and tries to have her run away with him and I'd probably kill 'em, too. But it's a shame what it did to the rest of 'em. That's his brother in a box. I see it better because him and Christian are friends and Christian says things. You see those boys hassling you, but you don't see Brandon when he's crying in his brother's bed because he misses the first friend he ever had. Or how it tears up his mama. Your sister left, but she ain't dead. Your daddy ain't dead. Try to think of what he sees, not what you see. You're the hero in your story. You ain't the hero in his."

The knife in Eric's pocket felt strangely heavy.

Yarrow led the way back to the admission gate, checked beneath both cash register drawers, then closed the window and locked it. He nodded along as if Eric had responded.

Eric watched him meticulously check the locks on each doorway and each window. He hadn't paid to get out onto the pier in years. Yarrow let the locals go out on it for free, said it helped business, that it kept the pier bustling and attractive to tourists, but Eric wondered if there was another reason.

Yarrow gave the window a tug to make sure the lock held, then turned to Eric. He gave him a hard, appraising look.

"Son, you spend too much time here. Go home. Clean yourself up. Get some confidence. Go and get a girl." He laughed at whatever he saw in Eric's face. "That part's easy, you know. Girls love confidence. That's all. Rest doesn't really matter. Even scrawny nerdy little shits can pull big catches. Don't just think things. Say them. Do them. They'll get wetter than—" he paused. "They'll like it. Get laid, finish up school and just... go. Coleridge ain't the world."

Eric wondered if someone had given Tiffany the same advice.

"Can you tell Christian to leave me alone?"

Mr. Yarrow shrugged, slipped the tobacco tin back out of his pocket and inspected it for a moment before popping it open and prodding around with his fingers.

"Sure. Might even listen. He's a good kid. But I'm not telling them to stop being friends and sooner or later the Anders boy will want to settle up. You're the only one left for him to blame. Boys do boy things. My advice? You stay away from them until you can get out of this place. That boy has lost a whole lot and he wants it back."

He tucked a final pinch of the tobacco in his mouth, put the tin into his breast pocket and then he pulled the gate shut behind them. He slapped the lock closed but didn't bother twisting the combination.

"Okay," Eric said.

"It's late. Get on home," Yarrow said. He headed off toward his salt-crusted, rusty Ford. The pick up looked comically small next to him and he had to fold himself up into the driver's seat, head ducked low. "Need a ride?"

"No."

"Should take a ride if it's offered."

"I'm good."

Mr. Yarrow shrugged, gunned the engine to life, and the truck trundled off into the night.

CHAPTER TWELVE:

The enormity of what Yarrow said didn't settle on Eric until he was halfway home.

He had pulled a knife on them. He had taken the blade out and had planned to... to what? To stab them for making his life miserable? If they had fought him, someone would probably have died. He could have killed them. He could have ended up just like his dad. And all for what? A handful of magazines and a torn backpack? A rock collection?

His mom's car was missing from out front. She must have picked up a shift at the gas station, he supposed. Home alone.

He didn't realize he was crying until he was stumbling through the front door, but he couldn't stop it, couldn't wipe away the tears that blurred his vision before the next wave replaced them. Couldn't stop the ugly throb of shame. His dad wouldn't have cried.

He did not go to his room.

He went down the hallway to his parents'.

He kicked aside the laundry baskets as he went, the lumps of rough, musty towels that would end up being nesting spots for mice, Eric supposed. He'd seen their little bodies scrambling around more and more often lately, the tiny rice-grain flecks of brown they left behind dotting the base boards and clustered in dusty corners.

He flipped the light switch, but nothing happened. The light-bulbs had been cannibalized for other rooms.

No great loss. There was nothing much to see. Nothing new, anyway. Just more disuse. More shame. More waste and wreckage, unwashed sheets and pill bottles, his mother's dirty underclothes strewn around. He tried not to look at any of it as he went to his dad's side of the bed. Not at the unmade bed where he'd once listened to his parents read simple books to him as he nestled between their warm bodies, not at the dressers his dad had sanded and stained a few years back, definitely not at the forest of family photos that sat on top of them. He didn't want to see the pictures. His mother, pregnant and dressed in white lace. His father proud in Army greens. A framed polaroid of a four-year-old Tiffany holding him for the first time, when he was still mewling and pink and messy from birth. The four of them smiling and sunburned at the beach near New Bedford. Younger, stronger, all full of life and hope. He didn't want to see their lie that things turned out happily ever after. The people in those photographs were dead.

He ran his hand along the back of the nightstand until he felt the nail his father had tapped into the wood, the key hanging from it.

He palmed it and headed to the closet.

The light bulb inside had been spared, blinked to life when he tugged the chain.

Behind the wall of button-down shirts and jackets, the great door stood—a gray behemoth with a brass wheel for a handle that looked like a part of a ship's helm.

He twisted the key in the lock, spun the wheel and the ponderously heavy door creaked open.

Inside, the hidden treasure. The secret heart of the room.

Wooden stocks, black plastic and polished metal. Rifles, shotguns, all in their narrow racks, muzzles turned toward the sky. Handguns, tucked in holster sleeves along the door. Glossy cardboard boxes of ammunition had been stacked up near the top, stamped with caliber numbers and illustrations of bullet holes. Perfect circles and their corona of silver, as if they'd punched evenly through painted metal sheets.

Not like a real bullet hole.

He pictured Matt Anders, his head come apart on the ground in a blackish smear of blood and brains and splintered chunks of skull.

The corpse.

The first shot went through Matt's sternum, blew out a hole through his spinal column the size and meaty red of a peach pit. The second shot caught him just above the eye as he dropped.

He'd seen the crime scene photos during the court case. The prosecutor had used them to show the cold-blooded precision of the violence and Eric hadn't been able to look away. That was the moment Eric realized—truly understood—that his dad was really going to prison.

He wondered if Brandon had seen the pictures too.

That boy has lost a whole lot...

Eric reached out and traced his fingers across the weapons one by one. He knew where he'd end up. The same one he always did. The last one in the line on the door, a simple little black box of a gun, the one the hero always seemed to tout around in movies when chasing down the bad guys. The one he had always imagined learning on, when he turned sixteen and his dad finally took him out to the range.

He wondered if his dad had stood there, some ten months before, choosing out which gun to bring to that bus stop when he went out to bring Tiff home. He tried to picture his father weighing each option. The revolver with the hidden hammer. The oversized, steely pistol the wide mouth. Then again, maybe his dad just grabbed the easiest choice. The gun didn't really count, when you thought about it. The bullet did. That was the part that ruined everything.

Eric was done with Brandon. He knew it in his bones. He didn't want to fight him or hurt him or pay him back for the past months of petty torments. Not anymore. He just wanted to be done with it all.

He was tired of being alone.

He missed Christian Yarrow treating him like a friend, and not something feral. There had been a time when they were inseparable. Chris had spent the night just about every other weekend. Eric's mom kept boxes of Captain Crunch in the cabinet with him in mind. They'd fallen out a bit over the last few years, but that was only natural. Chris had no aims higher than the trailer park. That had never mattered as a kid, but little by little Eric had come to realize that Christian sat far lower down on some bizarre social list, and those things that never mattered before, well, they were starting to.

Now he wished he could have it all back again.

As if he deserved anything.

He had always felt wronged by how so much of Coleridge had turned away from him for a crime he hadn't committed, but now...

He'd pulled a knife on Brandon. He'd wanted to hurt him. Not just hurt him. Kill him.

Tears came again, but a slower weeping, and no amount of shame could chase them away. He missed his dad. He missed his mom. He missed his friends.

No point in staying open for business if business is shit.

He imagined himself uncaging the small black beast, the cold heavy weight of the barrel, an anchor pulling him under. The bullets like stones for his pockets. The black tunnel leading down into the forever depths. No light. No music. Just cold.

Who would even hear the shot? Who would notice? His mother? Tiffany on her Tuesday calls when she wouldn't even speak to him? Would it echo in the slamming of cell doors and sirens or would he disappear altogether, a simple flicker of light in a star-spangled sky? He pictured R'hial cutting through the water. The expression on her face as she told him not to make her wait again.

Then he was finished crying and the feeling passed.

He set his father's knife on the shelf inside, next to all those unfired bullets.

He closed and locked the safe.

He returned the key to its hiding place.

He set everything back in place so that no one would notice his trespass—nevermind that no one would ever think to check—and when he was back in his room, he sprawled onto his bed, still fully dressed.

He fell asleep with his door still open and the light still on.

ric Ross, please report to the principal's office.

The intercom called his name and knocked him out of his reverie. He'd been drawing her again as he dozed through class.

His head ached and he had a difficult time recalling what the voice had said. He usually felt better the morning after visiting the gun safe, but his night had passed in a restless blur, consumed by dreams of his legs fusing together and of slipping into mysterious fathoms below. The sketch didn't just show her eyes or a vague approximation of her face. It showed her collarbones, her shoulders, the curve of her breasts and darkened nipples. The fullness of her lips and her odd cheeks. The proportions were damn close to perfect, the shading accentuating her into something almost life-like. He felt a momentary rush of pride before he realized what the intercom meant.

If he got roped into a meeting, he'd never get to the pier. They'd keep him late, or send him home or call in his mom and then it would all go to hell. He began shoveling his books into the plastic grocery bag that served as his backpack, even before the overhead voice finished dismissing them for the day. He stood up with the rest of the class and bolted for the door.

"Eric?" Ms. Grenada raised a hand. "If you wait up a minute, I'll walk you there. Don't worry, it's not…"

Eric pushed past her as if he didn't hear.

He could guess what they wanted to talk about. Maybe it was grades, maybe it was the showering thing. Maybe one of those three had mentioned the knife. Whatever it was, he didn't want to know. Didn't want his mother to know. Didn't want to deal with it. All he could think about was the pier, was R'hial waiting for him.

The rush of students made it easier for him to disappear, and for once he barely minded the occasional snicker, the slight distance as people pulled away from him for a moment before going about their day.

Down the locker-lined hallway, out the front door and into the sunlight.

Ms Grenada's voice called after him but he didn't worry about it.

He wiped at his face and he could taste the salt of his own sweat, his heart beat thudding in his chest. He didn't even slow down when he saw Brandon leaning against the brick wall next to the bike rack, dressed in his usual jacket and scuffed jeans. The other two weren't with him, and there were too many kids around for him to risk starting anything much. And for all he knew, Eric might still have the knife.

"Well if it isn't the wannabe school shooter. I was waiting for you, psycho-boy." Brandon announced.

He made no effort to stop Eric walking by him, though. Eric fiddled with the lock. He reset the chain in the gears, suddenly grateful that the older boy had never thought to ruin the bike. He turned and raised his hands, palms up.

"I don't want to fight anymore."

"Aw. Come on, killer. Don't you wanna pull the knife on me again?"

Brandon opened his jacket and whatever response Eric had hoped to throw together exploded into incoherence.

The black grip of a pistol poked out from Brandon's waistband. Eric froze.

Brandon held the jacket open a moment longer, made sure Eric got a good look, before closing it. The stream of other kids walking by gave no notice, continued on without a care in the world, unlocking bikes, lingering next to friends, heading to buses.

Brandon leaned back against the wall.

That was the reason he was alone, Eric guessed. The other two wanted no part of this next stage of the game. Or Brandon meant to shoot him and he didn't want his friends getting hurt.

His legs shook and he pressed his knees together to steady them.

This was how he was going to die. Brandon would wait until he climbed onto the bike, then it would all start. The gun out for everyone to see. The sound of shots. The screams of students and teachers as suddenly The Thing was happening, The Thing that every school rehearsed for, every parent dreaded, every student played out in their mind again and again.

He felt his lower lip tremble.

Brandon smiled.

The other students kept up their noisy parade, laughing, conversing, each doing their own thing, no idea that death was waiting just feet from them, and that it was *smiling*.

"I coulda told the teachers about your knife, you know. Got you expelled. I didn't. I can handle you myself. Fuck, you were really planning on stabbing me for calling you a fag? Something's wrong with you Rosses." Brandon grinned at the look on Eric's face. "You don't like to hear that, do you? But it's true. Your sister ran away, your mother's a drugged up whore and you bring a knife to school, wanting to kill someone because they called you on your bullshit. Guess you really are like your daddy. I wonder if he's having as much fun as you would, getting raped in prison."

Eric's sucked in a breath through his nose and let it out, then another.

The pressure built in his temples, pressed inward and he found himself baring his teeth at the older boy. Not fear, but fury. He had wanted to turn over a new leaf. He had paid his dues. He thought of Mr. Yarrow's words of caution but none of them made sense in the daylight, standing across from the person who was going to kill him.

He was going to die and this was going to be his last conversation. Not with R'hial under the pier. Not with his family. With Brandon fucking Anders, outside of a Coleridge fucking High. He wished his dad had brought enough bullets for the whole family. For the whole school. For everyone who had shunned him or sneered at him or turned away from him.

"You know what, Brandon? Fuck you. Maybe I am like my dad. Yeah? Well, how'd that work out for your brother? Think about that next time you're in his room crying for him."

Brandon flinched, a stunned flush creeping up his neck to overtake his face.

Eric freed his bike from the rack and wheeled it off. As he pedaled, he braced himself for the sound of gunfire, the wasp-sting of bullets tearing into him, but there was nothing. Just the crowds and the voices and the grind of the half-flat tires.

He pedaled faster and faster until the school dropped behind him and he rocketed out across split sidewalk and salt-pitted asphalt, his legs churning, the adrenaline bursting through his veins in a hot rush and suddenly he was laughing, shaking with it, teeth bared and grinning and he wanted to clap and jump and howl to the sky above.

The world blurred past and the pier widened in front of him. He kicked off his shoes before he reached the first step of the Suicide Steps.

She was waiting in the water below.

CHAPTER FOURTEEN:

He sat on the metal-capped wood, his selection of gifts laid out on the broken piling beside him. Ocean spray leapt and bit at his ankles, a sharp and unrelenting cold. She rested on her elbows on the broken piling, her nose only inches from the things he had brought.

He hadn't been able to bring much. The plastic grocery bag had held one of Tiffany's old notebooks and little else, but he managed to lay out a lighter, a laminated map from last year's history class and a necklace he'd grabbed up from his mother's nightstand, some cheap metal chain and brass heart-shaped brooch. All the nicer jewelry had been pawned off.

R'hial inspected them one by one, a broad grin on her face.

"Gifts," she said.

"Check this out," he said. He picked up the lighter, rolled the spur and a tongue of flame shot up. She let out an audible gasp. She held out her hand and he passed it to her. She flicked the spur. Nothing. She tried again a few more times, then shook it and set it down. She watched it as if expecting it to move. Then she picked up the map and inspected the flat, undivided blue of the oceans.

"All wrong," she informed him.

"It only shows the land parts. They don't know about... underwater stuff."

She shrugged and set it back down.

She poked at the necklace next. Whatever value Eric's mom put on it was gone, now that it was far away from her. In R'hial's hands it was just a scrap of metal junk. He wondered why his mother had kept it, what it became when she held it. Maybe it had been some teenage gift from childhood crush or maybe it reminded her of some special moment of her childhood that only she remembered. He shouldn't have stolen it, he realized. R'hial held it up and let it sway like a pendulum for a moment, and then went back to the lighter.

Eric watched her and fought the sudden urge to reach out and touch her hair. Instead, he gripped the metal cap beneath him, pressed his fingers against it until they ached.

"Can I ask you something?" he asked, at last.

She nodded without looking up, her chin coming to rest on her cupped hands. Alongside her neck he could see the slits of gills flared open, a reddish mesh hidden beneath. He shivered.

"Were there others?"

"Others?"

"Did you have other friends? Like me."

"Friends..." she considered the word. "No. Not friends."

She flicked the metal spur again, but with no more luck.

"Why me? You've been here for... well, forever. Why now?"

She set the lighter down on top of the map. Then she turned her face up toward his. Her eyes were wide and dark and sad. When she spoke, she spoke slowly.

"One day all will be silent. No dock. No pier. No music. No boy with gifts. No…" she gestured at the map. "But I will still be. Father says never talk to landmen. No good." She shrugged. "But I like you. You saw me and come down. You are good talker. I like talking."

Eric thought of his room, the peeling posters and filthy clothes and the deafening silence of empty space no longer meant for living. He spent day after day at the pier, clinging to the light and life of it all. How could he blame her for doing the same? For wanting something better than a drowned existence down in the dark? For finally having enough?

Wanting was a terrible thing.

Don't just think things. Say them. Do them.

"I like you too, R'hial. Do you still want me to go swimming with you?"

The water looked horribly cold and he was not at all dressed for it. All he had to wear anymore were sweatpants and tee shirts. He wondered if he'd end up with hypothermia.

She shook her head.

"No. Too cold for you. All clothes." she gestured at him. "Maybe soon."

"What do you want to do, then?"

"The pier," she whispered.

Not a smile on her face, but something closer to anger; a terrible and wild hunger. It reminded him of his mother eyeing the medicine bottle, of his father bellowing at Tiffany over the dinner table when she came home late.

"How?"

"R'scylla says…" she shook her head. "Maybe. Tell me about it?"

Eric chewed on his lip for a moment.

"It's the same as always. R'hial, they say no bodies ever wash up around here. When people drown or whatever. That they never have. Is that you?"

She said nothing. She pushed at the necklace with one jagged nail, scooting it back and forth across the metal.

"Why do you take the bodies?"

"I keep. Just keep, not kill. A… collecting."

He had a sudden mental image of her dragging a corpse, the head and spine shot out, down to some hidden grotto. A new souvenir to pack away among a forest of mossy skeletons, their jaws gaping and withered bone reaching up as they settled into thick, slimy mud. His neighbors. The good inhabitants of Coleridge who strayed too far into the water, all gathered in some nightmare pit in the darkness below. Somehow, the thought seemed worse than her simply killing. He wished he'd never asked.

"But you did kill him. That man. Didn't you? Is that why?"

"You said you are not caring."

"I know. But…"

"No. Not for collecting."

She glanced back at the water behind her. She would be going soon, he knew. He hadn't heard the distant sound, yet, but he could read it in her posture just the same. He'd seen Tiff sneak out enough times to sense it. He shifted, felt the crinkling of paper in his pocket.

"Oh! I have one more thing for you," he said.

He shifted on the piling as he pried it out of his pocket, then held it up to her. The drawing from class. She stared at it, face slack with wonder. She reached up and touched the page, slipped it out of his hands to examine it. She bent the corner and held it up to the sky. Her fingers smeared the ink where they touched the paper, warped it with their wetness.

"If it gets wet, it'll fall apart. But that's okay. I can always make more. It's not great yet, but I—"

She shushed him. She studied the smear. Then she dipped her hand into the water and wiped her fingers across the tail he had drawn. The scales that he had painstakingly detailed for the majority of sixth period dragged into an indistinct blur.

"I'm still working on those," he said.

She turned to him and color flickered in shooting stars across the dark of her eyes. She gripped the piling where he sat, pulled herself up to him, and pressed her mouth against his.

Not a gentle thing.

A hungry kiss, filled with the taste of seawater and copper, her mouth open as if to drink him in. Needle edged teeth scraped against his lower lip. Her skin was cold and the water soaking into his clothes made him shiver as he gripped the piling for balance, palms to metal. The naked shape of her pressed against him through his shirt and she gripped the back of his neck to pull him closer. For a moment he understood that he couldn't pull away from her if he tried. That she could tear him apart if she chose to. Her thumbnail rested lightly against his throat, the webbing fanned against his skin.

A rush of warmth flooded through him and he leaned into her, let go with his hands to hold her.

The water rumbled in response. The distant call, only this time it sounded closer. Angrier.

She slipped away and dropped back into the gently rocking waves and he barely managed to keep himself from tumbling in after her.

"Again," she whispered. She left before he could find his voice, before the memory of her body had faded enough that he could think clearly, and fled into the open water. She did not take the gifts. The picture lay stuck to the pillar beside him, crumpled and soggy and unrecognizable.

"Again," he said to no one in particular.

CHAPTER FIFTEEN:

He wasn't going back to school.

He knew that when he woke up. Part of it was Brandon and the gun. Part of it was threat of meetings, of the principal's office and the well-meaning pity as they informed him of some new way his world would become more miserable. Most of it was in the memory of salted lips, the glitter of emerald scales, the otherworldly glimmer she wore like a halo.

It was a Friday, so he didn't have to worry about his mother. Work needed the extra shift on Fridays, so she wouldn't be back until long after school let out. Instead, he set about getting ready.

He showered for the first time in weeks, flicked the ancient crust away from his mother's shampoo bottle before squeezing a dollop of the pearlescent slick into his hand. He scrubbed his body in water hot enough to leave his skin stung pink, and then climbed out.

No clothes were clean, of course, so he reused his underwear and headed to Tiffany's room where he found a pair of her jeans. They clung uncomfortably tight against his legs, but he doubted anyone would notice. The pockets had been stitched shut for some reason, but he doubted anyone would notice that either.

Next, he snuck into his mother's room. There was no one to hear him, but he still crept in on quiet feet. The overhead was still out, but sunlight streamed against the curtains and filled the room with a gentle glow. With the dark pushed back he found himself almost able to pretend his dad was back in the Army, coming home soon. He hadn't been born when his dad had deployed, but it was easier to stomach than the truth. The stern-eyed man watched him from photos as he slunk past to rummage through their dresser.

The envelope took him several minutes to locate, crammed beneath neglected, threadbare underclothes in the top drawer. It was creased and nearly flat, contained two ten dollar bills and a handful of miss-matched pills that spilled out among the forgotten scraps of tattered lace and cotton.

He knew his mother kept a stash of money in the drawer. He couldn't remember who told him, but it had always been an understood back up—if there was an emergency that was where he could find money. Was that really all that was left, though? The great collection of the Ross family value. He grabbed one of the tens and tried not to think about his mother looking for it later.

He ate a bowl of stale Cheerios in front of the blank television screen and waited for his nerves to settle. When that didn't help he tried doing a few pushups, but they just made his elbows hurt. He went and got a shirt from the floor and combed his fingers through his hair and then he couldn't think of any more reasons to delay.

At noon he climbed onto his bike and pedaled off toward the grocery store over on Wopanaak, a short ride from the beach.

He stepped through the front door feeling more like an adult than he could ever remember, the ten-dollar bill clenched tight in his fist. His last stop before he went to see her. On the overhead, some old guy sang about the summer of '69 being the best days of his life and Eric found himself humming along. He wondered if the guy was still alive.

He rooted around the flower section, a few sparse handfuls of flowers sprayed wet and wrapped in folded cellophane. All of them were somewhat wilted despite the blast of air conditioning units and open ice boxes. Roses with their carefully pruned thorns and curled velvet petals came in near twenty dollars, but the artificially bright carnations were only six so he grabbed them instead and headed for the front. He grabbed a Sky Bar and ate half while he waited for a register to open, the gooey centers of the chocolate thick in his mouth. He saved the other half for R'hial, just in case she wanted to try.

He was so distracted that he didn't look at the cashier until it was his turn.

Mrs. Anders looked back at him for a long moment, the conveyer belt grinding quietly along and the man on the overhead still warbling. Eric had met her before a handful of times, through his sister's involvement with the Anders boy. He'd always thought she was pretty; blue eyes and a bright smile, the scrollwork of tattoos arching up her arms and down from her collarbone. She looked different, now. Her lips had gone thin, her cheekbones sharp and bird-like. Blonde bowed its head to gray. Her manufactured smile slipped away while he watched, those bright blue eyes turning damp with tears. No anger. Anger would have been easier. She simply looked as if his presence had doused her good mood and left miserable coals in its place.

"Thank you, Mrs. Anders," he said, once he'd found his voice.

She opened her mouth, closed it and swallowed. She nodded to the display. Eight dollars and ninety-seven cents. He passed her the ten and left without waiting for change.

His bike lacked a basket and he still had no backpack beyond the cheap plastic grocery bag, so he tucked the bouquet under one arm and clamped it tight to his side as he wheeled out of the parking lot.

His pulse began to speed up as the pier grew in the distance, the Ferris wheel spokes poking up high above the flat skyline.

He wasn't sure why he was so excited, but he *was* excited just the same. A Christmas eve sort of anticipation, a thrilling, heart-wiring readiness that charged through him like lightning. He didn't know what he hoped would happen, but he simply sensed that today was the day for it. That, like the man in the grocery store song, it was now or never.

His legs ached as he pedaled, flat tires grinding along over sand-dusted blacktop and scraps of beach gravel. Ocean breezes tugged at his hair and tousled it, left his face feeling strangely dry—although he supposed that may have been the shower. The cliff overlooking the beach stretched to either side, and he turned toward the pier. For a moment he simply marveled at the forest of pilings below and the titanic weight they carried.

He chained his bike up in its usual spot, grabbed his bag and headed over toward the beach staircase. The pier itself hadn't yet opened for the day, but it would soon. Somewhere up there, the carousel horses were champing at their bits and waiting for that first alarm, the reel of music, the promise of lights holding their own against the night. The thought brought a smile to Eric's mouth. The cellophane wrapping under his arm had grown clammy with sweat and he stripped it off of the flowers.

He paused a few steps down and tucked the bag in among the stones, his phone inside it. He kicked off his beaten sneakers, relished the race of his pulse as his feet gripped the cold wood.

"Girls love confidence," he recited.

Without letting himself hesitate, he tugged his shirt up over his head and added it to the heap, and there he stood, dressed in just his sister's abandoned jeans.

The chill of the air set in immediately, wind licking up and down his bare skin and causing tiny hairs to prickle. He flexed stiff hands, swollen already, and picked up the bundle of carnations from where he'd laid them. He wished they didn't look so puny, some dozen green-stemmed sticks with their garish plumes. He wished he had somehow bought the roses. Something properly red instead of the dyed pink. Something real, something vibrant, something full of life. Something to make her gasp.

He picked his way down the last few stairs, waterlogged wooden boards creaking in submission beneath his bare feet. The temperature plummeted with each step. Unclenching his jaw took a concentrated effort.

You're the man, now.

Girls love confidence.

He tried to summon the feeling he'd had at the top of the stairs, but his excitement had soured, had tattered and fled to dark corners of his gut and left an aching absence in its passing. Instead,

he simply pictured himself—a shivering, skinny pale boy with a handful of dead flowers and an embarrassingly sparse tangle of hard curled hair that started at his navel and crept toward his jeans. Something feeble. A fraud. A very cold fraud.

The pier loomed overhead, the monolithic pine risers like the pillars of a cathedral, and he squinted down the shadowed tunnel between them, waiting for a first sight of her. He was earlier than ever before, he reminded himself. He might have to wait hours. Some part of him hoped he would. High above, the radio coughed into life and began belting out a song halfway through a note.

The telltale glimmer of green flickered out among the darkness and he tightened every muscle he could muster to fight off the jitteriness.

She had come back. She had seen him, met him, *kissed* him and she still came back.

She swam closer, drifted on her back down the barnacle-toothed aisle with languid, razor-edged ease before turning toward the beach. Her eyes opened wide and she examined him with an exaggerated slowness before she let out her odd, wild laugh. She smiled and raised a hand.

He waved the flowers in return.

Her smile vanished. The playful green glow choked into slate gray and she dropped back into the water with barely a ripple to discern her from the roiling surf.

"R'hial?" he asked.

She wasn't the one who answered.

"Well, well, well. What the fuck do we have here?"

CHAPTER SIXTEEN:

Brandon's voice.

Eric's heart gave a vicious squeeze, seemed desperate to push warmth through his scrawny frame despite the leeching grip of the air. He turned to find the three of them heading down the steps—Brandon, Christian and Handsy. The whole crew.

Christian whistled.

"Going for a swim? Jesus. It's cold as balls out here."

Brandon let out a snort and grinned.

"With flowers? Nah. Our boy Eric is here for a girl. So how about that? Where's the girl?"

Eric shot a look up and down the beach but besides the four of them, only rocks and shadows and waves kept vigil. The pier up above was silent. If R'hial was watching, he couldn't spot her.

"Fuck off, Brandon."

The pretense of a smile faded. Christian and the Norwegian stepped out to either side of him. Not that Eric would be able to run anyway. He was barefoot and shirtless and there was nowhere to go. His bladder felt suddenly tight. An instinctive electricity coursed through him in waves, a remnant of a time when mammals learned that running was the only thing that kept you breathing.

"You'd like that, you little cocksucker. Saw you biking around outside my mom's work, but I didn't see any girl. Where is she? Bet you she'll be a good girl for me. Bet you I'll have anything I want from her."

"Leave me alone."

But he knew they wouldn't. He was already alone, already isolated. The carnival music reeled on above. No one to hear. No one to see. Just him and them. Brandon stepped closer.

"Leave you alone? Like your daddy left my brother alone? You're the one who pulled a knife on me. Well, where's your knife now? Didn't see it at the top of the stairs with the rest of your shit."

Christian snorted. "Dude. Put a shirt on. Whole thing seems kinda gay."

Handsy kicked at the filthy blue tarp and the stones holding it down. The polyethylene sheet let out a wet crinkle and a cloud of gnats circled over their disrupted breeding ground in a frantic, buzzing blur.

"Hey, look at this. Could almost use it like a bed. Maybe he's planning on sucking some dick like his mom. You know how she earns those oxys, right?" Handsy shoved his tongue against the inside of his cheek until it tented outward, then grinned at Eric. His neck was banded with ugly red sunburn.

Eric hoped it hurt. He tried to build on the feeling of anger, but mostly he just felt shame. He hoped R'hial wasn't nearby. He didn't want her to see.

"I don't want any trouble," Eric mumbled.

"Yeah. Yeah, I guess you don't," Brandon said. "Matt didn't either. Then your daddy went and shot him in the head. You want to tell me I'm gonna end up like Matt again? Come on, you little faggot."

"Brandon—"

He grabbed the flowers out of Eric's hand and threw them on the ground. Petals fluttered in the air, caught by the breeze, intertwining as they scattered down the beach where they clung to wet stone.

"I don't have the gun, either. Not today. It's just you and me."

And the other two, Eric thought, but he didn't say it. The beach stretched endlessly, empty in either direction. They were going to hurt him. They were going to really hurt him. He should have brought the knife, for whatever good it would do him. Maybe his dad's gun. Something.

"Talked a lot more shit last time," Handsy said. He didn't sound all that confident.

"I'm sorry," Eric said. He didn't know what else to say.

He crouched down to pick up what was left of the flowers. Maybe he could distract them. Maybe he could run. Brandon stood over him, his lip curled in disgust.

Women love a confident man.

He prayed Mr. Yarrow would lean over the edge of the pier to spit, see what was going on, do something to interfere. But of course he wouldn't. The pier wouldn't be open for hours and there was no god that cared. No one to hear him scream.

"Sorry? Yeah, I don't give a shit about you being sorry, Ross. That doesn't do a thing for me."

The urge to run flared through his mind again. It should be dark. It should be night. People didn't get hurt during the day, right? But they *were* going to hurt him. He knew it. They knew it. The secret was out. He just wondered how badly.

...sooner or later the Anders boy will want to settle up.

"Are those skinny jeans?" Christian snickered.

"Chris, come on," Eric said. Christian looked away. As if that negated the late-night sleepover conversations on the floor of Eric's bedroom, the jokes and school lunches and years of friendship. He turned to look at Handsy. The blonde boy scratched at his sunburn and then shrugged.

All that wishing to have everything back, all that wanting, those were stupid wishes of a silly child. Eric felt his strength seeping out him.

"No one is gonna help you, Ross. You brought this on yourself."

Beneath the bundle of artificially green stems a tangle of discarded fish hooks clustered, knotted together at their base by a clear cord. The same trash he'd seen on the beach countless times before, that he'd taken such care to avoid. Eric let his fingers ease over them, felt their needle points like strange thorns. He made his decision without thinking.

Eric lunged forward, shoved Brandon, and swung the barbed steel bouquet across his face.

Brandon let out a bellow of pain and staggered back.

Eric turned to sprint up the beach, but Christian and the other boy were standing too close and he hesitated too long because then he was on his on his ass and his whole world was back on the Tilt-a-Whirl, spinning in a madly reeling race.

"Motherfucker," Brandon slurred. It came out *Mu'urfucker*.

Fish hooks studded the older boy's face, looped metal hoops through his cheek, his lips, his nose. One jabbed up into the corner of his eye, the metal tip disappearing somewhere beneath, and not reemerging. Blood spilled from his pierced face, speckled the ground as he shook his head. The hooks glittered, swung like Christmas ornaments. Eric wondered if it had actually punctured his eye or just his eyelid, but he was pretty sure he knew the answer.

Brandon kicked Eric onto his back. The air shot out of Eric's lungs. He rolled onto his side, tried to curl up into a ball as the boy raged above him. Brandon climbed on top of him, fingers groping and gripping until they found their way around his wrist and bent it up behind him, rolled him over so that his face pressed down into the cold wet gravel and sand.

"Please don't—" he managed to whimper and then Brandon wrenched his arm.

It grinded and popped as his elbow dislocated, an audible sound like a chicken bone twisting out of socket. His vision fell into dull, muted grays. The boy continued twisting and Eric felt the bones shift, tendons stretching. An awful red blade of agony sheared up through him. Grit and shards of pebbles dug into his bare skin, frozen nails bruising his ribs, his belly, his battered face.

The pressure on top of him lifted and he tried to wriggle away. He only made it a few feet before Brandon put his foot on the back of his head. Not stomping or kicking, just pressing down. For a moment, he was simply relieved the older boy had stopped hitting him.

"I'm sorry," he tried to say, but no words came.

He gulped, gasped, tugged at unyielding air.

The first wave spilled over him and that was when he realized the childish games had entered uncharted space. Icy cold, wicked and brutal, rushed across his face, down his throat, filled his lungs as he gurgled and bucked and tried to scream. The wave retreated. The rush of salt and foam poured in a mucus slick out of his nose as he fought to catch his breath, to beg for Brandon to let him up. To tell him that it hurt. That it was over anyway, that none of it mattered. That he just wanted to go home and see his mom.

The froth had barely pulled back when he heard the roar of a second wave coming and then he was under again. He knew he needed to hold his breath, but his body didn't seem to care or respond. The others hooted and laughed. Warmth spilled down his thighs as he pissed himself.

A third wave.

A fourth.

The shoe relaxed before the next wave came in.

"Come on, killer," Brandon said.

Hands dug into his armpits and hoisted him up and Eric fell against his tormentor. He clung to the older boy, shaking with absurd gratitude, a simple gratefulness that he hadn't held him there until he drowned.

Short, sullen waves rushed around his ankles and he choked and vomited into the gray surf. The acidic burn of bile surging through the spigots of his mouth and nose set him retching again. His muscles felt paralyzed, refused to obey any attempt to find footing of his own.

He was moving. Brandon was dragging him.

It took Eric a moment to process that they weren't heading back to shore. The water came up to his knees now, the skinny jeans soaked and heavy as manacles around his legs. The breath he could find came shallow and stung in his throat. He sputtered and belched and gagged, sea water still spilling out of him, the salt scraping as it did. The sky leaned crazily overhead, clouds exploding like plumes of gun smoke, thundering carousel warhorses crashing into battle against the blue.

Christian was yelling something to Brandon as the two waded in after them.

"Come on, dude. Dad said we should leave him alone. We found him, you trashed his bike, you kicked his ass. Let's just go. It's goddamn cold."

"He'll fucking drown."

Handsy's voice, Eric guessed. The words were difficult to follow above the roaring in his ears.

"Won't matter, will it?" Brandon said. He wasn't yelling back to his friends. He was asking Eric. "Not like you're gonna wash up. Gonna take you nice and deep and let the water do the work."

Eric tried to resist but his wounded arm was anchored to his body by searing wires that throbbed with each step Brandon took. The water came to his hips, now. Then his ribs. Then his shoulders. Waves spilled by, the water tugging and bucking far more than the usual placid pace.

He struggled to keep his head up as the water rushed by in crests and valleys. As he tried to make sense of the words. Brandon was going to drown him. Bodies never washed up. The thought had an otherworldly quality to it.

He realized he had never really been afraid, before. Not really. Not all those nights, dreading his dad's upcoming trial. Not his fear of the dark, of those gory movies, not of his family falling apart. This was different. Even the gun was different. Those were all possibilities.

He'd passed into certainty. It was *happening*. He was dying here and now and things weren't going to be okay and he would be just another chunk of rotten green driftwood dragged down into the sea. He wanted to scream or cry but it wouldn't do any good. The water was reaching his neck and even though he kicked and struggled against Brandon, the effort was all no use.

The sky above blurred into the dull horizon.

He would never see his mother again.

Something pushed against his leg, skin like cold, rough leather.

He kicked at it, as it passed, unable to make any sense of what exactly had brushed him.

Brandon let go and Eric slipped under for a moment, bounced off the soft sand and pushed himself up to the surface, his head tilted back to keep above the waterline.

A hideous triangular fin cut through just an arm's reach away, water tugging along as the shadow of something terrifyingly huge passed between him and the shore.

Christian screamed, then, his voice climbing to an absurd, girlish octave before choking off into a gurgle. A second fin knifed by Eric, another cold body scraping past him as it joined the fray. The sunburned boy dropped into the water next, a soundless violet plume blossoming where he had waded only moments before.

Brandon was howling, shrieking as he tumbled toward the rocky shoreline. Eric hopped along the bottom, flung himself toward the beach with everything he could muster, tried not to think about the sharks, about teeth slicing through tendon and meat and ripping him out into the deep. Tried not to think about the churning bursts of warm color in the water like so many fallen carnations.

Brandon had made it most of the way to the shore when he turned to glance back, and for a moment Eric could see his round-eyed terror, the way his face had been peeled half off so that the muscle tethers of his jaw were exposed, the jut of yellow cheek bone and chin, the ugly pearls of blood-stained teeth. For a moment Brandon didn't look at him with hatred, barely seemed to recognize him as anything other than a fellow human being. He reached out in a desperate plea for help, the sparkle of fish hooks still dangling from where they had impaled his face.

And then she rose from the shallows between the tall boy and safety, her hair flaring around her in flickers of green bioluminescence, face twisted in predatory glee. A chunk of flesh hung from her jagged teeth, a pale and dripping banner, and Eric realized it was Brandon's face. The triangular fins cut in a loop around her. Rivulets of water and blood clung to her nakedness.

The water guttered with verdant light and when Brandon slipped under, she did too.

Eric pushed past, through the frothy mess, desperately heaving himself along with the one arm that would work. When he reached the beach he collapsed and rolled up, away from the water, the stones and sand digging into his numb skin. Pressure, not pain. Even when they dimpled his skin sharply enough to cut through, there was little blood. He fought to breathe. His teeth bit down of their own accord.

He was dizzy. The world was a sprawling dark tunnel, the pain of his dislocated elbow the only thing keeping him from blacking out.

And there at the end of the tunnel he saw her, as he had beneath the pier. Her light flickered and dimmed and faded away. She looked back at him, down at the blood covering her body, and then she hurled herself back into the sea.

CHAPTER SEVENTEEN:

He walked, half-naked, as his shadow grew behind him. His arm dangled loose by his side. His hair was plastered in a mess of dried mucus across his face.

His phone and keys were gone. His shirt was gone, along with his socks and shoes and anything else. Had there been a candy bar? He had a hard time remembering if he'd stopped to look for the things he'd brought with him, but then remembered he'd circled back twice to check and if he went back again, he might not have the strength to try for home again.

They had thrown his stuff among the rocks, or out into the ocean.

And he had killed them.

His feet were a mess of blood and he tried not to look down. Seeing the split toenails, the gravel and grit embedded in the wet, weepy trenches of scrapes and cuts only made it worse. He didn't feel it anyway. The blacktop was cold and he was still numb from the water.

His jeans clung to his legs, and each step came as a struggle.

He shambled along, pace after pace. Again and again he saw the torn face looking back at him. That last flash of helplessness. Of desperation. Not hatred. In his last moment, Brandon hadn't wanted to hurt him. He had been afraid. He had been terrified and he had wanted Eric's help.

You ain't the hero …

Most of the cars he'd seen pass had rocketed by without so much as a glance. And why would they? He hadn't even tried to flag them down. The ones who slowed down, he slunk past, snarling like something feral without quite understanding why.

It didn't matter.

One step, then the next.

There were things he should do. Find a house, any house, knock on the door and ask for help. A store, even. Anywhere at all. But what good would it do? Brandon walked alongside him, clutching his open face and screaming.

…ain't the hero…

The only place to go was home. He wanted to see his mother. It seemed entirely possible the whole thing had been some fabrication and everything might be alright when he got home. Maybe his dad would be there too, and Tiffany, and they would all watch a movie together on a couch that hadn't yet turned filthy and there would be no ocean in it, just boys on bicycles riding the moonlight. No one screaming as they were murdered.

The sun was beginning to dip toward the horizon by the time he stumbled onto Maple Park, the blacktop giving way to sidewalk and then to tall grass. He was dreaming long before he reached the doorway.

When at last he pushed his way through the doorway, he realized it wasn't Brandon screaming. It was his mother.

CHAPTER EIGHTEEN:

is mother strapped him into the passenger seat of the Nissan and he reached out and held her hand as she drove. A slow, itchy warmth returned to him as the miles passed.

He blinked and he was sitting in one of the plastic chairs in the hospital waiting room. He had a shirt on, the crumpled foil of a space blanket draped over his shoulders and pulsing with sweaty heat. When his feet brushed the cheap blue carpet they stung, but then he was being pulled along by his mother, her arm wrapped around him, squeezing him against her bony frame. A cold linoleum hallway later he was in the check-up room and first one nurse was asking him questions, then another. The world blurred around him in a hectic, senseless spin, a carousel of sights and sounds. Questions that he couldn't answer. Posters with faces that ranged from smiling to frowning. Glass jars of cotton balls. Gloved hands touching his skin, touching the parts that hurt the most. The crinkle of a paper sheet on a leather bed. The squeeze of a blood pressure cuff, constricting like a snake, then the hiss of it relaxing. Bright lights for him to follow with his eyes. More questions.

Can you hear me? Do you know where you are? Do you know what happened to you?

The ride slowed.

Brandon's screaming ghost vanished and the vertigo left with it and all at once Eric was simply tired, instead. Just so tired. He cleared his throat.

"I fell," he said. "I fell down the Suicide Steps."

His mother let out a strange sound.

"The what?"

The nurse nodded. She seemed satisfied by the answer. A tattoo climbed like ivy up her neck, but the words on its petals were senseless to Eric. Names. Dates. Memorials for the dead, maybe.

"Over by the Bay Point? Yeah, we get one every year or so. Be glad it's not broken. Be glad it's not your neck."

The nurse read off a few more questions—do you know what day it is? Do you know your home address?—and then they set his arm in a sling and they bandaged his feet. They prodded him awake each time he nodded off. At some point a police officer tried to ask him questions, or maybe it was a nurse, but Eric wasn't sure because when he opened his eyes again he was home in his bed.

The sun was up. A breeze streamed in through a window that hadn't been opened in months. He hadn't noticed the smell in his room until now that the fresh air had pushed it out and replaced it. His bed and clothes were soaked with sweat and clung to him as he sat upright, but his room smelled *clean*. He reached around with his uninjured arm to check his phone but his phone was of course still gone. The clock radio said it was almost eleven. His injured arm was strapped into a sling that was beginning to chafe his neck and his elbow gave a dull throb as the pain awakened too.

His mother had dragged the old childhood rocker into a corner of the room and sat in it, snoring, her hands folded across her stomach as if in prayer. For the first time Eric could remember, she looked old. Not just unkempt and scrawny, but wearing down. Just about worn out. The pretty girl from the pictures in his parent's room was just a bittersweet memory. Her hair was graying at the edges. Her face shaded in lines. Her chin sunk down to her chest and he could imagine her decades older, shuffling around in slippers, her body trembling and liver spotted and weak from age. For the first time, Eric really understood that there would come a day when she was dead and gone.

A bowl rested on the ground beside her, filled to the brim with a brothy yellow soup, and all at once Eric was so hungry it hurt.

She grunted, tasted the air and eyed him for a moment before realizing he was awake too.

"Hey, mom."

"Hey, babe. Good morning," she blinked at the open window and wrapped her arms around herself. "The soup's cold. Sorry if it's not very good. Sorry for… for everything. I know I've been struggling a bit. I'll be better really soon. I promise. I just… I don't know what I'd do without you. You're all I have. You scared me."

She offered him a weak smile as she set the bowl on the nightstand.

The soup had separated, the cool surface dotted with yellow pools of oil, but Eric took it with the one hand not trapped in a sling and he drank it, poured it down his throat until it slopped along his chin and he had to wipe his face with his still-damp t-shirt. The shirt boasted an Army logo on it. One of his father's that she must have grabbed for him.

He tried to apologize for the mess, to tell her that the soup was great, that he loved her, that he understood, but his throat was too full and he was afraid that if he spoke he'd start crying. He reached out and gripped her hand instead and she kissed him on the forehead.

"Thanks mom," he managed.

"I love you, Eric."

He closed his eyes and slipped back into sleep, but for a moment he imagined it was R'hial who said it.

CHAPTER NINETEEN:

r. Marty's voice woke him up from a tangle of senseless dreams. If the man had knocked, Eric hadn't noticed. "Eric? Enough, Jenny. Eric. There you are."

Eric blinked back his confusion as the door swung open and the two walked into his bedroom. The sheriff was dressed in his service blues, gun in holster, and no part of him seemed at all like the gentle, cheery man Eric had known growing up.

"Mr. Marty?"

"I need you to tell me what happened to those boys."

"Marty, he's been through enough. Eric, you don't have to answer him," his mother said. She latched onto Mr. Marty's arm to pull him back but the sheriff shook her off.

"You damn well do have to answer me. Brandon Anders is missing. Christian Yarrow and Aesir Hansglavadsson too, all last seen in his company. We found Brandon's car near the pier where you hang out—"

"Lots of people go to the pier," his mother said.

"Enough, Jenny. We found Eric's wrecked bike there too. And his shoes. And his shirt. Someone threw them out among the rocks. What happened to you, Eric? What really happened?"

"He said he fell down the beach stairs."

"Jenny, if I want your opinion I'll ask. I'm talking to the boy."

Eric licked his lips, drew his knees up to his chest. His arm ached at the movement. "I fell down the Suicide Steps."

Brandon's face, punctured with metal coils of fish hooks, mouth gaping, flesh peeled back from his teeth.

"You're lying." He paused, stared down at the boy. *Christian's terrified squeal as teeth ripped into him, as his life spilled out into the cold water just a matter of feet from shore.* Eric tried not to blink. He hadn't even seen Handsy's end. Just the blood. "A staircase didn't twist your arm like that. It didn't trash your bike, either. I know you had trouble with those boys. This is bigger than that, though. Did you go to school on Friday?"

"He did," his mother said. "He fell down after school."

Eric shook his head. He tried not to see his mother's expression. "No. I didn't."

"Where did you go instead? Walk me through your Friday."

"I just... I was hanging around. I went to the store. I don't know. Then I went to the pier and..."

Brandon had looked him in the eyes the moment before he died. He hadn't spoken a word. Helplessness and terror needed no language. Bile surged up Eric's throat and he narrowly choked it back down.

His mother clapped her hands together. "Enough. Is anyone under arrest? Any warrants? No? Then get out. You're trespassing. Anything he says to you won't stand up in court."

"Goddamnit, Jenny. I'm not trying to arrest him. I'm trying to find three missing boys. I'm trying to figure out if they're alive. Eric was seen at the grocery store buying flowers. The beach is covered in flowers down by the pier." He turned toward Eric. "Why were you bringing flowers there? Anything to do with the naked woman?"

Eric said nothing, so Mr. Marty bulled ahead.

"You know. That woman you were so curious about. The one who the fisherman said committed murder. Coincidence is one thing, but this is evidence. Who is she?"

Eric looked past the sheriff, out the window and down Maple Park Road. Out that way, far out of sight, was the beach. The only thing he could make out was a plume of sand and dirt waggling after a distant truck as it careened along the main drag. He tried to organize his thoughts, but none of it made any real sense. None of it would convince the man. There was no way he could put the sight of R'hial tearing the older boy apart into words, even if he had been willing to try. She had saved him.

"I didn't hurt them."

"Fine. Then who did? Are they alive? Listen, I have five missing people now. In one goddamn week. One on Sunday, one on Tuesday, three on Friday. The parts I keep coming back to are the beach, this mystery girl... and you. If you don't help me, you aren't just covering for a friend. You're an accomplice."

"Tuesday?"

"He was with me on Tuesday," his mother said. Mr. Marty paid no attention.

"What, you didn't know about that one? You sure have a line on the others though, don't you? Don't treat me like I'm stupid.

Tuesday night, a fifty-four-year-old man was out metal detecting on the beach a mile or so away from the pier. Never came back. Left his detector next to his coat, then... what, went for a swim? He was a Navy boy, maybe he went to go help that girl in the water. I don't know. You tell me. You skipped that day at school, too."

Eric shook his head and stared out the window instead. In the distance, he could make out the shapes of a small parade of cars and trucks careening down Wopanaak. One pulled off, light glinting off the windshield like a winking star.

Had she killed more? Why? Nothing he said was going to help. His mother drifted toward the hallway, backing away from the scene that he supposed must have felt all too familiar.

We find the defendant guilty...

The truck was familiar too, he realized. A salt-frosted pick up, and no longer some far distant shape. It turned onto Maple Park and came barreling down their street, bounced over the curb and then pounded through their mailbox with a sledgehammer thump. Huge divots followed the truck's path through the pulverized tall grass. Green juice dripped from the rusted fender.

"The hell?" Marty muttered.

He squinted out the window as Yarrow climbed out and stomped over to the door. He didn't knock. The door crashed against the wall as he kicked it open.

Marty faced the doorway, hand on gun, as the huge man barged in. The sharp, bitter smell of whiskey billowed in after him.

"Eric? Where you at, boy?"

"Woah. Sir. What are you doing—"

The big man towered over Mr. Marty, stared down at Eric as he crowded his way into the bedroom. His eyes were bleary and bloodshot and he reeked of vomit and booze, some distilled essence of the Bay Point given human form. His massive hands clenched and released every few seconds as if he didn't know how to still them. Or as if imagining them around Eric's throat. "Where's Chris, you little shit? Where's my fuckin' kid?"

"Mr. Yarrow, I'm going to need you to calm down—"

Yarrow shoved his way past the sheriff. Eric shrank away toward the far side of the bed.

"And I'm gonna need you to shut the fuck up, pig. He knows where my boy is at."

Then both the men were bellowing and Eric's mother walked back into the room.

Clack-clack

She raised the shotgun, stock to shoulder, the blue steeled barrel swaying as she aimed it at Yarrow's chest.

"You stay away from my son, you trailer trash hick." The sudden silence made Eric shiver. "Get the fuck out of my house, or I'll kill you. Right here, right now, with the sheriff watching. This will be the last moment of your miserable, shitty life."

Mr. Marty raised his hands, palms toward her.

"Jenny, put the gun—"

"If I want your opinion, I'll ask for it. Marty. You get out too. Both of you. Out of my house and away from my boy. You understand me? He's all I've got."

"Mom?" Eric's voice cracked. His mother didn't look at him. The shotgun stayed aimed at Yarrow.

"You gonna stop her, Sheriff? Or she suck your dick enough times you'll pretend she didn't just say that?"

The sheriff kept his hands raised. "Get out of her house. I'm gonna do everything I can for you, but you're drunk and breaking into an innocent—"

"Innocent my ass."

"—an innocent woman's house. Get out. Now."

Yarrow looked between the two of them, ignoring the shotgun trained on his chest. He spat on the floor before turning to Eric.

"You, boy. I took care of you. You owe me. Tell me what happened to my son. Your friend. At least... at least tell me if he's alive. Is he alive?"

Eric felt tears building up. He tried not to remember Christian's squeal of pain and stupefied terror, how girlishly high it came out. Christian had told Brandon to stop, hadn't he? The memory was all muddled.

Marty watched, waiting for an answer too.

The big man's lower lip trembled as he seemed to read the truth of it in Eric's face; his chest hitched with a sudden hiccup that came out partly a sob.

"Now," Eric's mom said. "Out."

She clicked the safety off and eased her finger onto the trigger, and Eric remembered his father lecturing him about gun safety in the same room only a couple years before: *Keep the weapon unloaded and the safety on. Keep your finger off the trigger. Only point at something you're willing to completely destroy.*

Only, Mr. Yarrow had already been destroyed.

The man let out an animal bellow of frustration and stormed past Eric's mom, back the way he'd come. Eric watched him stalk across the lawn, kick at wreckage of their mailbox, and then climb up inside the truck. Tires spun as he jerked it into reverse and careened off the lawn, down and out of the neighborhood stretch. The smell of whiskey lingered behind him in the room.

Marty let his hands lower to his hips. He tucked his thumbs in his belt, kept his hand well away from the butt of his gun.

"I suppose I don't need to tell you that you only get to pull that stunt once. I should take both of you in. Eric and you." He shook his head before Eric's mom could protest. He ignored Eric entirely. "I'm not going to. What you're going to do is help me. I am going to need a statement from him. I know he didn't kill five people in a week. Those boys damn near killed him, unless I miss my guess. But I need answers. Real answers. You told me before that he wouldn't help me, and maybe you're right. But he might do it for you. If he doesn't, he's going to be looking at the kind of trouble I can't get him out of. Talk to him. And then bring him to the station. Jenny, either he comes with you, or he goes with me."

"This isn't like Jack. Eric didn't hurt anyone. He's just a kid."

"We all were, once. This can't wait on pride. On grudges. There's a murderer out there."

"Tomorrow. We'll be in at the station tomorrow morning. No lawyer. He'll tell you everything. I'll… I'll talk to him."

Mr. Marty chewed on his lip for a long moment before he answered.

"Don't make me come back here and get him, Jenny. Don't make me cuff Jack's boy, too."

"I promise, Marty."

He scrubbed a hand through his thinning hair.

"Guess someone's gotta go check on Yarrow. Make sure he doesn't run himself off the road. Christ this is a mess."

He picked his hat up off the kitchen table and tucked it onto his head. He gave Eric a long, piercing look before he headed out the door. Only when the sound of car engines had faded into silence did his mother set the shotgun down on the coffee table next to the pill bottle and her car keys.

Eric climbed out of bed to watch her as she stared down at the table. His arm ached in its sling, but not as badly as he'd thought it would.

"I didn't hurt them," Eric said.

His mother glanced up at him, frowned as if she had forgotten he was there at all.

"It doesn't matter. We're leaving this shithole. This town. This life. Up and out of here. Tonight." Her tone brooked no argument.

He had never loved her more. Tonight. The idea was intoxicating. But...

She sank down onto the couch and looked between the keys and the bottle of medicine. He could see her deflating, the beaten, weary version crowding its way back in.

"We can't," Eric agreed, as if she'd spoken it out loud. "I need to..." but he couldn't tell her what he needed to do. He didn't know it himself. He thought of R'hial but all he could picture was Brandon screaming, his face ripped open. How the salt of her lips could as easily have been the taste of blood as of the sea. She had saved him, but was that really enough?

"We can. Tomorrow morning," she amended. She shook two pills out and swallowed them dry. Then she closed her eyes and took a long, slow breath. "Tonight we'll rest up. We can leave tomorrow. And you're never going back to that pier."

He nodded, even though she couldn't see it.

Even though he knew it was a lie.

CHAPTER TWENTY:

Eric waited in his room until she had fallen asleep and then he headed out.

He had no bike to get him there quickly, but his mother wouldn't surface anytime soon to notice him missing. One pill put her under for hours. Any time she doubled up meant she'd be out until morning at the earliest. He tucked her in beneath the blanket before he left, the shotgun resting on the table beside her, and headed out the front door.

They weren't going to pack up and leave, he knew. Not really. There was no way to leave Coleridge. No way to leave the bottle of pills, the mess, the decay, the pier. The shadow chasing him every evening he faced toward home. A mouse might as well dream of leaving a trap.

The sun turned golden, gave way to a molten slab on the horizon behind him as he trudged along, his arm nestled in the sling. He could move his fingers, but each step sent a bruised jolt up to his shoulder and before the first mile was through, he found himself gritting his teeth. The evening was cool, quickly turning toward cold, and he wished he'd grabbed a jacket. Winter was coming on fast, bulling its way through the fall before summer had fully passed.

He smelled the ocean long before the horizon opened across the water. With each step, the raucous scream of gulls became more pronounced, the tug of wind pulled harder, the light grew a little dimmer. Rain clouds had gathered, too, but he ignored them.

The pier was dark.

It was one of the first times Eric had seen it that way. Even the colder months, when the rides where closed and the stands and stalls were all boarded up, the lights stayed on. They were a matter of pride. The Bay Point Pier was a symbol of Coleridge, far more than any townhall or main strip.

Now it looked dead. A corpse. Dead, and waiting for him.

A feeling of wrongness swept over him, grew stronger with each step. The beach was haunted. How could it not be? The last time he'd been there, three boys had walked out and never come back. He wondered if he would see them down on the shore, waiting, their corpses mutilated and waterlogged, bloodless wounds gaping to show their cored-out insides. The unending hate in the pulpy pits of their eye sockets, urging him on one more trip down the Suicide Steps where they would crawl over him, onto him, into him.

By the time he reached the top of the steps he was shaking. Opening his eyes to look took a concentrated effort. There was no trace of Brandon or the other two.

Instead, he found her.

Halfway up the stairs.

"R'hial?"

He wondered how long she had lain there, slumped across the steps. Her hair hung limp and ragged against her face, plastered there with sweat and sea water, the color beaten out of it by the dull twilight.

She squinted up at him. "Eric? You left me."

Her voice was rough, dry, the melodic lilt turned to rasp.

He wanted to tell her she was wrong, but he knew it was a lie.

"I'm sorry. I was scared."

"You said you'd always come back." She shook her head in accusation. "You didn't. I saved you. I *needed* you. And you left. It... hurts, Eric."

She gestured at her legs with one hand. The webbing of the fingers had been pruned back, cut and hanging in flaps between her fingers. The claws had been worn down to nubs.

"Oh god..."

Her legs. She had actual legs.

Of a sort.

They were nothing like his. Nothing like anything he'd ever seen. A hideous cobbled patchwork of flesh, poorly fitted puzzle pieces sewn together with fishing line and fraying, braided strands of hair. Knobs of misplaced knee caps and off-angle bone peeked through the weeping gaps, and where her legs met together...

Eric gagged, grabbed at the stair with his good hand. He did not remember sitting down.

"I'm... monster," she said.

"R'hial," he whispered. He put his hand on her shoulder, tried to look anywhere other than the ragged mutilation. Her skin felt slick and hot but she shivered at his touch. Her lips were gray. "What did you do?"

"I just… I wanted… and then you left. I had to try…" but words failed her. Her eyes were wide and dark as they looked past him toward the boardwalk above. The ethereal glow was gone. The only thing left was empty space. "You can go again."

"Come with me, I'll get you home. My mom can help." A ludicrous claim. Even if she hadn't been drugged out of her mind, there was nothing she could do. Nothing anyone could do. That R'hial had survived the replacement at all was a marvel. "How…?"

She shook her head. "R'Scylla. All went wrong. R'Scylla said bring legs, so I bring them. I bring many, but not the right ones."

"The right ones?"

He knew what she was going to say before she said it.

"Yours."

"Why mine?"

"A sacrifice. Important ones. Not just…" she gestured at the carnage. Trickles of pink water leaked from the open lipped scars between the mismatched blocks of meat—all the shades of the pebbles on the beach below. One wrinkled patch showed the scrawling of an anchor tattoo. Some pieces he almost recognized—Christian's dark tan, a paleness that could easily have been Brandon. A sunburned strip. Others he did not. Any of them could have easily been his own.

Eric thought of the towel balled up and wedged beneath the fridge, the cutesy stitched-in slogans all sodden and stained.

The most important ingredient is love.

Nausea swept back over him.

"Wait here," he said. As if she had a choice.

He climbed down the stairs, heedless of the cold, until he found the tarp. He smoothed it as best he could, brushed off the grit and flecks of blackened seaweed and tiny swarming bugs. He couldn't do much for the smell, but it would have to do. He dragged it up the stairs and draped it over her. A trip back down and he returned with the yellow ribbon of plastic crime scene tape. He wrapped it around her middle as best he could manage and cinched it in place.

It was easier when he didn't have to look at the mess.

"Come on, R'hial. We'll fix this. We'll get you to a hospital, and they'll..."

He didn't finish the thought. He put his good arm around her shoulders and helped guide her to her feet.

She leaned against him, nearly causing him to pitch off the steps as she struggled to support herself. Each step looked like a marionette's crude imitating of walking, her legs bending in strange geometries beneath the tarp as she jerked and flopped along. Most appalling of all was how it *worked*. Eric tried very hard to not look at the shapes beneath the blue fabric. To not think about what she had attached and what she had removed. Bile simmered in the back of his throat.

They could make it work. And why not? She'd need a wheelchair. Legs like those were never going to work all that well, but so what? He could take care of her...

He made it to the top of the stairs before he realized there was no way home. He had no phone. No bike. Nothing. Home was nearly three miles away and she'd barely made it up a flight of stairs. He wasn't so much better off either.

No chance of that.

Night had fallen and he hadn't even noticed until it was too late.

He turned instead toward the Bay Point.

CHAPTER TWENTY ONE:

The entry gate loomed over them, belted in a stainless-steel chain, the pennants at the top snapping like uncoiled whips in the fitful gusts of the coming storm. The gap between the doors looked out onto rows of shadowy shapes, hulking in the starless dark.

Eric gave the combination lock a tug and the it sprang open. Mr. Yarrow never did like to change the code. He unhooked the chain, and the two of them hobbled through, arm in arm, out and onto the abandoned pier.

He knew it was a mistake almost immediately, but there was nothing else to do.

The only sound that greeted them was the howl of the approaching storm. The only life was the swaying of cheap buildings pushed by spray-flecked wind.

The Bay Point Pier was a ghost town.

The pair lurched together past booths and gaming sheds—dart throws and the hammer strikers and ball tosses, water racers and roulette wheels—their joyousness absent in the dead of the night. They looked cheap and tired and old—toothless, geriatric mouths gaping in senile smiles. Nothing more than old repurposed food stalls that offered neither nourishment nor comfort, only a momentary distraction. The glass-faced popcorn cart was a greasy, empty cage.

The rides were no better. The Ferris wheel towered over the whole pier from its place at the far end, a lifeless, looming thing that rocked in the wind with mumbled protest. The cups of the Tilt-a-Whirl sat still and empty. The carousel's mirror-walled center no longer refracted crowds and bustle and a frantic clutch at a contented summer sigh. They reflected a betrayal. A lie. R'hial looked at each in turn, face slack with disbelief. The storm clouds grumbled dark promises above.

She clung to him, arm damp and slippery around his neck, the smell of the discarded sea heavy in her tangled hair and reeking from the tarp. The two staggered forward the last few feet. He collapsed next to her on the Lover's Bench. The dead carousel waited, in front of them.

Tears trickled down her face. Her lower lip trembled in a child-like pantomime of disappointment. He put his arm around her and tried to find the words to comfort her. Life was like that, he wanted to tell her, but he couldn't find his voice.

Wanting was an awful, pitiless thing.

It wasn't fair. She had only wanted music. Light. Life.

"Wait here," he said.

As if she had a choice. He smiled at her, but she didn't look up.

An ungainly hop got him over the metal cordon that separated the carousel, and he made his way to the control podium.

He ran a hand underneath it until he found the key, slotted it and twisted it. He kicked the wedge against the pedal and hit the green button, the way he'd seen Mr. Yarrow do countless times before.

Nothing.

Not even the lights. No power.

Of course.

He stepped up onto the carousel track and between the files of chipped plastic beasts, the dull fanged tigers and silently screaming horses, the dragons and serpents and unicorns and gryphons with cracks showing the gleam of rebar skeletons that held their bodies together beneath the gilded, flaking paint.

He tried the half-hidden door at the center. It swung open.

A smell of cigarettes and booze and musty oil, a stuffy garage stink that made Eric think of long-legged spiders and their hollow prey, strung up like decorations. He could just barely make out the breaker box. Thunder grumbled as he cranked the metal door panel open.

He groped across the ranks of greasy switches, praying nothing bit him until he found the switch and flipped it on.

Light blazed on around him, the speakers let out a feedback shrill, and then the carousel bell rang and spilled into its carnival reel of music. Helixes of dust spiraled down past the overhead bulb as it swung in the wind and only then did Eric realize he wasn't alone. Mr. Yarrow snored softly on the floor a few feet away, a bottle in his hand. The tiny cot looked like little more than a pillow beneath his head. The big man grunted at the disturbance, rolled, and slipped back under.

He no longer looked so intimidating. Eric hoped his mother was sleeping just as peacefully.

Eric crept out and closed the door to the inner chamber and stepped between the slow stampede of mechanical mythologies as he headed back over to the bench where R'hial sat, her eyes wide with wonder. He sat beside her.

"It's not much—"

She shushed him with the sound of a quietly breaking wave, and so he didn't say anything else.

The lights danced reflections in her eyes as the ride turned, turned, turned. Somewhere, the timer was going down. It would all stop soon. For a moment, though, it was enough.

She rested her head on his shoulder.

He prayed the music would last, but far too soon the creatures slowed and fell still, the music choked off as it waited for another press of the button to start it cycling again. The two sat watching the lights and Eric kissed the top of her hair.

That ugly thrum from before sounded, cut across the open ocean and resonated through his bones. Not the quiet murmur he'd heard previously. An angry roar.

She stiffened against him.

"What is it?"

But he already knew the answer.

"He's calling me home. My father."

CHAPTER TWENTY TWO:

The storm broke open in force before he could get her to her feet.

Massachusetts gales came in heavy and howling and this was no different.

An icy spatter of raindrops rattled down as they raced inward from the ocean, across the deck, and overtook the two. The wind, no longer content to tug at the banners and tents, hurled itself in a wild stampede, the kind of storm that had left widows at home for centuries. Eric gripped at the bench to force himself upright. The planks beneath his feet shuddered with the force of the waves below.

The door to the breaker room swung open, slammed against the mirrored panel beside it hard enough to leave a spiderweb of cracks, and a moment later Mr. Yarrow stumbled out. He squinted up at the wavering Ferris wheel and the clouds the color of woodsmoke, then he turned toward Eric. If he was at all surprised to see him, it didn't show.

"The fuck is going on out here?" he bellowed over the storm.

When he noticed the girl huddled beside him on the bench, the man froze.

"The fuck?" he asked again.

"Mr. Yarrow—"

A crash of thunder rolled through, so loud that it hurt. Eric worked his jaw, ears ringing as waves roared by and shook the pier.

The thrumming sounded again, close and furious, the vibrations throbbing in Eric's gut.

The storm surged in reply.

Rain hammered against the wooden planks, slashed like frozen bullets against them. The Ferris wheel let out a tortured groan and they all turned toward it in time to see the lights flicker and the bulbs pop one by one. An ugly electric whine filled the air.

Mr. Yarrow sprinted back in to the breaker box and then darkness spilled across pier. The shapes of the rides reduced to dim silhouettes traced by flashes of lightning.

The Ferris wheel leaning, one flash. The next, it tilted impossibly far under the barrage of wind and rain. Metal tore and wood splintered as it bent and bowed and only then did Eric understand it was happening, actually happening, and the boardwalk planks below him jumped.

A sound like a twin gunshots rang out as the wheel's anchoring tore loose. The massive wheel wavered, dipped, and then it spilled over.

It hit the ocean below with meteoric force.

Eric dropped to his knees.

He struggled to form any thoughts beyond a blank disbelief. The Bay Point was supposed to be invincible. It had always been invincible. He thought of the wedding picture on his mother's nightstand—his parents arm in arm and smiling—but he wasn't sure why.

The next flash of lightning traced the wreckage of the wheel, half submerged and leaning against the pier. Massive chunks of splintered wood jutted up where the Bay Point had held it. Matching black pits yawned where the pier had torn away.

Mr. Yarrow dragged himself across the carousel, pulling himself from animal to animal, his yellow oilskin coat flailing and jerking in the breeze and for a moment Eric could only think of those fishermen who had founded Coleridge with their blood and sweat. The helplessness and terror they must have felt, caught out in the open ocean.

"We need to get you out of here!" the massive man bellowed.

The wheel tilted further in its sunken grave, leaned more heavily against the pier's frame.

R'hial's fingers dug into Eric's injured arm and he found his footing. He steered her toward the gates, step after shuffling step.

"Eric," she said, but he couldn't hear the rest over the storm.

He gripped her tighter against him, her skin bitterly cold and slippery from the rain. It felt like gripping an armful of surf. She leaned in close to his ear and for a moment he thought she would kiss him.

"You need to go. You need to leave me,"

He shook his head. "Mr. Yarrow will help us home, it's just a storm."

"It's my father."

Something struck the pier and the entire structure shuddered beneath them, the very ground heaving as the pilings below bent and splintered under the strain. At the far end, one gave out. Then another and another, each pillar's falling causing the next in its line to slouch and drag under into the froth. The carousel tilted as the planks below it weakened.

Mr. Yarrow stumbled, flung an arm out for support but there was none to be found. He made it a half step toward Eric when the ground split open beneath him.

One moment he was there, the next he was a darkened blur slipping into a gaping, splintered maw.

Eric let go of R'hial, pushed her toward the shore, and then crawled toward the brink. He stopped short as he passed the bench. The pier ahead was no longer a bridge, but a ramp down into the gnashing water where far more than waves circled. Monstrous shapes and angry-angled fins hacked through the gray surge, illuminated from behind into hideous proportions by flickers of dull, angry green. Roiling, serpentine bodies. Hooked tentacles groping blindly upward. Mr. Yarrow did not come back to the surface.

The remains of the pier shuddered again, the moment's reprieve used up. Eric felt the boards bend and go slack beneath his feet and he scrambled back, his fingernails digging into the cracks in the slippery boardwalk to heave himself along. Something gave in his elbow, an echo of the pain from before, and then he was clinging to the Lover's Bench with his one good hand.

The pirate ship ride hit the water next, and then the pier began to fall apart.

The bench tilted under his grip. He climbed over it and dropped down against the far side, but then he felt it begin to slide. He kicked and clawed and snarled, finally pushing himself up to his feet as he charged upwards. The entire pier was going in, he realized. No way around it. It was time to go. Flickers of green blasted through the ocean, a strobe of submerged lightning crackling furiously through the waves as the storm surged to a fever pitch.

He took off running, as best he could manage.

The popcorn cart lay in a halo of shattered glass that crunched under his feet. Closer to the entrance, the gaming booths bent and wagged under the onslaught.

As he passed, the Tilt-a-Whirl toppled into the surf, the supports beneath it too weak to hold it upright, and then he was thrown flat, his wounded arm unable to keep his chin from hitting the wood. He rolled, pushed himself back up to his hands and knees and crawled forward only to find a gap.

The ride spilling over had torn the Bay Point in two and left him stranded on a pitching island of wood. Across the gap, he saw R'hial standing near the gates, looking back at him. He reached out for her, but she did not come. She shook her head and fled, step by hobbling step.

Eric hoped she made it. He looked back across the ocean.

A wave was rising, a wall of dark water seething as it crested. The center of it flickered with the peculiar glow he'd seen flow through her eyes, through her hair, that firefly gleam magnified into a runaway flame, a seething green wildfire from beneath. The emerald writing of a clock radio counting down time.

A new pair of eyes looked back at him from the wave. A face full of terrible rage. Massive shoulders split the surface. The wave rose higher.

There was nowhere to go and nothing left to do, so Eric did not run. He did not fight. He thought of his father and he did not let himself cry or beg.

He simply stood and waited.

Time ticked away, second by second, until there were no seconds left and then the wave reached its peak and fell, dropped like a hammer.

His world exploded and the bitter sea consumed him.

CHAPTER TWENTY THREE:

aude Grenada hurried into the ShopMart, head bowed against the storm. The air conditioning inside rushed around her, crept cold fingers down her neck and beneath the raincoat. The dull fluorescents that hung above the aisles gave a warmthless greeting.

"Awful weather tonight," the cashier mumbled. He didn't look up from his phone.

Ms. Grenada nodded to him.

He wasn't the usual cashier. She felt a pang of shame that she knew which cashier usually manned the register, and when. She knew which stores were open this late on Sunday nights, too, and it wasn't the first time she'd braved a storm to get there.

Smoking was an awful habit.

Her students could never know about it. She was supposed to be a role model. Most of them had enough bad habits anyway.

She grabbed a red box of popcorn from the aisle to make herself feel less desperate, then stood and waited while the conveyor belt creaked along, as if there was any sort of line.

The shame and self-disgust didn't keep her from chewing on her lower lip as she eyed the rack of cigarettes like a gambler eying the odds board. She knew what she would get, but the sight of all those glossy, cellophane boxes still thrilled her with a strange, hungry sort of awe.

"Tareytons," she said. "Two."

Cashier nodded, grabbed them and tapped the sign to see Maude's license, as if the creases at the corners of her mouth weren't a good enough indication of her age.

On the radio, The Wallflowers lamented a broken headlight.

She'd been teaching long enough that she rarely even thought of herself as Maude. Just an echo of what the world around her called her. Ms. Grenada. There were worse things, she supposed, but it still seemed peculiar. She'd felt so much enthusiasm for the job, once. Becoming Ms. Grenada had seemed so important.

These days she seemed to build most of her enthusiasm around the half-pack before bed, cuddled up next to Mindy, her calico cat, some tensionless Lifetime movie playing in the background. Mindy would lick at the salt from the popcorn, at least, even if most of the bowl went to waste.

Then back to class in the morning. Another day, another week of dressing up as Ms. Grenada.

She wondered if the Ross boy would show up. Not that it mattered now, that opportunity had sailed. She had saved some of those weird drawings he did and sent them off to MassArt, begged them to send a representative. She'd figured that might be what the boy needed. They'd agreed. It wouldn't help him with a career or anything, but it would get him into the school if they were impressed, and it might help him get a scholarship. Headmaster Burke had reluctantly agreed to be a part of the process—no one really wanted to help the boy too much, considering what his dad did—but then the boy went and skipped the meeting and ran off and hadn't been back since.

It felt like all her life was caught in the same loop of trying, of pouring out, and of the world just wiping it away. Unlike most of the faculty, she wasn't born in Coleridge, she came from up in Rockport and had taken the job as a sort of civil service idea. To help the helpless. Only later did she discover that she never learned how.

By the time she swiped her credit card, the night sky was still. In the few minutes of her shopping, the storm had vanished as promptly as it had come, all that violence gone to waste. Rainwater still hung in pebbles on the foggy windows, wandered in streaks through the condensation.

Bells jangled as the door swung open.

"Awful weather…" the cashier began and then trailed off as the girl stumbled in through the door.

A tarp was wrapped around her like a discount princess's gown, a yellow plastic sash cinching middle, and that distracted Ms. Grenada for a moment from the realization that there was something off about her. With the pallor of her skin, the too-wide, too-dark eyes and the dull, dripping hair. With her legs. There was something very wrong with her legs.

The girl—or a woman? It was hard to tell—took two lurching steps into the store and stood on the welcome mat, damp and muddy water trickling down from beneath the tarp and leaking out onto the floor in an ugly, pinkish pool. She stared at the lights, at the aisles, the rows of food packed in neat boxes and bags, focusing on them one by one as if they were something entirely alien. She tilted her head and nodded along to the music for a moment. The Wallflowers continued to warble on.

An alien, Ms. Grenada thought, and for the first time in her life the thought wasn't something silly. But of course not. The woman was just… disabled, somehow. Homeless. Another part of Coleridge in need of saving.

Her heart fluttered as the woman's attention finished with the aisles and slowly settled on her. Hurt, maybe, although she seemed not to notice.

The woman shambled forward, wobbling and jerking, her knees jutting out through the blue plastic in all the wrong places, causing her to bounce with each ungainly step. Like a newborn horse, Maude thought. She'd loved horses growing up. There had been something so unfailingly wild about them. Her teeth were digging into her lower lip again, she realized.

The homeless woman stopped in front of her and leaned forward to peer at the box of popcorn. The smell of her was a physical force, a powerful, beachy stink of salt and rot and something that made her think again, for a moment, of the Ross boy.

Maude held the box of popcorn out to her, tried her best to keep from trembling.

"It's already paid for. You can have it."

The woman's hands were a mess as she reached out to take the offering. They looked like someone had glued plastic between her fingers and cut it away, deeply enough that they sliced into the mesh of her hand in weepy red lines, or maybe she had gloves half-melted to her hands and had tried unsuccessfully to remove them, but no matter. She tugged the box into her arms, oblivious to what had to be unfailingly painful.

The cashier was silent next to her. He stared fixedly down at his phone, kept his eyes to himself and his mouth shut. He did not dare look up.

When the woman smiled, Maude was the only one to see the bristle of needle-thin teeth.

EPILOGUE

lo waited by the doorway to the ShopMart, hoodie drenched and cold and clinging to her frame, as she watched the bleeding woman dance.

The storm had let up, but violet clouds still hung heavily in the night and the air had a bitter cut that would only grow worse in the coming months—although in Massachusetts the bite of winter was never that far away. When Rick had tucked a twenty deep into the pocket of her jeans and sent her out from the RV down on Pleasant Oak to go get him a pack of Marls, the wind had been screaming like something wounded, the frigid rain slashing in an iron studded drumroll that stung her face and tasted like salt as it soaked her to the bone.

Flo didn't mind. She liked the cold and the dark.

There was a power to the night in Coleridge—maybe to the night everywhere, but Flo was only eleven years old and hadn't made it much farther than Main Street. There was a strange, subtle magic in being alone among the gnarled, knobby pines, in walking across asphalt swept so clean by the rain that it caught and tore the scant moonlight into glittering ribbons; a nebulous power in seeing small dark shapes slinking away from the approach of an unfamiliar intruder and in the straggler few locusts that dared to set up their clamor despite the quickly approaching October that would kill them one and all. She could feel it even in the shitty ShopMart parking lot, with the sand-eroded blacktop punctuated in scraggly weeds that crept through the cracks.

Like leaks in a sinking ship, she imagined, and could almost hear Rick's snort of contempt.

That was the part about walking at night that she liked the best. No Rick. She could pour her imagination out into the world without anyone judging. God only knew why her mother had invited him into their lives. He spent his time avoiding work, and she spent her time avoiding him. Especially after dark. She wrapped her arms tighter around herself.

And sometimes, every so often, the night seemed to reach out and offer something back.

One time she'd found a hundred dollar bill pinned under a stone by a light post, fingerprints stamped on it in a rusty stain. Another time she saw what she thought must have been a wolf pass the road, some hulking dark furred shape that paused to stare at her with predatory, human intelligence until her mouth dried and her heart hammered in his chest and her thoughts devolved into the basest primeval response—*Run Run Run*—before it slouched along into the dense thickets of roadside pine.

Tonight, the bleeding woman danced.

At first glance, Flo thought the lady was having a fit. She'd seen that Emerson boy have a fit before. A seizure, she reminded herself. Her mother was a nurse and had been very firm on the distinction. But there was a rhythm to the way the stranger flailed, her movements struggling to keep time with the muffled warble of the store's radio.

She was dressed in some filthy blue boating tarp, belted in crime scene tape, and she should have looked ridiculous but there was a wildness to her that kept Flo fixed in place.

The woman spun and twisted, flung her hands above and around herself, her face set in a clenched smile with each twirling, lurching step down the aisles of mundane canned goods, packets of Rice-a-Roni and Hamburger Helper and brightly colored ten-cent ramen. The woman clutched a box of popcorn in fingers hooked into claws. Behind her she left a trail of blood.

The bleeding woman stumbled and caught herself, nearly pitched into the neatly stacked display of Campbells soup and then she laughed, threw back her head and shouted out the sound, but it held no real humor. A strange, ugly and defiant bark that sent Flo's heart stammering—*Run Run Run*—and the woman danced on to the beat as if she could hear that too.

Two left feet, her mother would have said, but there was something more to it that Flo simply couldn't wrap her head around. There was something off with her. With her feet. Not just the swaths of watery red surf they smeared behind her, either, and not the mud caked up her ankles that hid them half from sight. *Two left feet.*

The woman moved faster and faster, her movements turning frantic, arms wheeling in a fumbling, cartoonish pantomime of imbalance, the scuffed linoleum dancefloor thick with spattered grime and uneven foot prints, all reds and browns—the colors of clay, of life and warmth and new beginnings and other things that Flo had nearly forgotten.

All at once it ended.

Her legs gave out and the bleeding woman tumbled, crashed into the display at the end of the aisle and collapsed into a heap. Soup cans clattered around her and rolled through the mess, leaving twin-lined tracks as they strayed on their dented treads. She did not stand. Did not even try. She simply lay in a huddled heap beneath the tarp, one hideously stitched ankle protruding, blood still dribbling down from somewhere farther up. Her body shook, but Flo wasn't sure whether it was more laughter, or tears, or simple exhaustion.

"Hey! Out. Out the door," the cashier bellowed, waving a hand as he approached, a mop hoisted like a spear in the other. Fucking Brett. Flo hated catching him on shifts. He always made her uncomfortable in a way that she couldn't quite define. His scraggly beard spilled down onto his neck and shivered as he swallowed. He was always swallowing, always sweaty, always looking somehow damp. Even through the glass Flo imagined she could smell him.

The woman rose to her hands and knees, her face twisted with anger, the filth smeared on her cheek like clotted war paint from where her head had struck the floor, but then she slipped and went down into the muck again and the fight left her just as quickly. She dragged herself toward the doorway on her hands, legs trailing, still clutching her popcorn. Brett followed a few steps behind, holding the mop out in front of him. He pressed the mop's shaggy head against the door handle to shove it open, and a rush of processed, stale-smelling air spilled out into the night along with the burst of soulless radio pop and the jangle of the bells strung up above the door.

"—and stay the fuck out. You come back here and I'll call the cops. Christ," Brett muttered after her as she pulled herself onto the sidewalk and flopped down onto her side like something beached. Her beath came in short, shallow gasps. He wiped a sleeve against his forehead.

"Brett?"

"Flo? Christ. Fuck, what are you doing here? Could've gave me a goddamn heart attack, creeping around out there. I swear, don't you people sleep? Goddamn lunatic here wrecking the store and this weather is just awful."

"Pack of Marlboros."

He looked at the woman on the ground, then at Flo. He sighed and reached up, pushed the security camera above the door to a different angle, and wiped sweat from his forehead with the back of his wrist.

"Twenty," he said.

Flo fished out the money and handed it to him and he headed back inside.

Then the two of them were alone, her and the bleeding woman. The night made it hard to tell much of what she looked like, and her hair hung in a shroud halfway across her face, but behind it, her eyes were wide and dark and watching Flo with a sharp and hungry attention that had nothing in common with her clumsiness. Flo thought again of the wolf.

Run. Run. Run.

In the distance, thunderheads rumbled. The storm hadn't fully passed through, Flo supposed. Just the first wave of it. She hoped it'd hold out until she got back home. The woman cocked her head and frowned toward the distant beach. It was too far to hear the waves, but she listened anyway, as if to a distant song.

The only music Flo could hear was the store's radio as the door swung back open and Brett handed her the pack of cigarettes. He did not offer her change.

"Thanks Brett," she said.

He waved her back with a grunt. "Stay away from that one," he muttered, nodding his head toward the bleeding woman. He didn't chance a direct look. He slipped back inside and closed the door firmly after himself before he put the mop to use.

When Flo turned back, the woman was standing. She had dragged herself up the concrete bollard that kept the parking lot at bay and now slouched against it, watched her with an unmistakable curiosity.

"Fuck you want?" Flo asked, trying her best to seem intimidating. She wished she sounded older, hated the low drawl in her voice that all the kids who went to school properly seemed to have shed. She sounded like Rick. For a moment she wanted to spit the taste out of her mouth.

The bleeding woman considered it for a moment before responding. "Home," she said. "I need a home." The answer was so openly bizarre that Flo simply stared at her, all pretenses forgotten.

"Me too. I mean, I have one but my mom left and Rick..." she trailed off. She couldn't imagine why the woman would care about some kid's problems—only the woman *did* seem to care, had taken a half step toward her, and the attention was anything but comforting. The woman wobbled as she stood, her bloody bare feet sinking into a puddle that had to be ice cold. She didn't seem to notice.

She's getting ready to chase you. Run Run Run.

The thought sprang up and Flo struggled to push it away. The woman could barely walk. She wasn't a danger. She couldn't be. Her mother always said that a nurse's job was to help.

"You got anyone to call?" Flo tried to imagine the woman making a phone call but the idea seemed silly. She was wearing a tarp for a dress. Flo doubted it had pockets. A nervous giggle escaped her. She wasn't supposed to talk to strangers, was she? No matter what her mother would have done. Not all of the night's offerings were gifts. "Do you have anywhere to go?"

The electric glow of the store behind the woman cast her features in shadow, but something inside the gloom flickered green, glittered and pulsed like a flurry of distant stars and then it was hard to think clearly, hard to think about her mother or the danger of night or even Rick waiting back at the trailer. She felt herself nodding in agreement before the bleeding woman answered.

"With you."

Made in the USA
Middletown, DE
22 March 2025